It All Begins with Jelly Beans

It All Begins with Jelly Beans

NOVA WEETMAN

Margaret K. McElderry Books
New York   London   Toronto   Sydney   New Delhi

MARGARET K. McELDERRY BOOKS

An imprint of Simon & Schuster Children's Publishing Division

1230 Avenue of the Americas, New York, New York 10020

Text © 2019 by Nova Weetman

Originally published in Australia in 2019 by University of Queensland Press as *Sick Bay*

Jacket illustration © 2021 by Federica Frenna

Jacket design by Rebecca Syracuse © 2021 by Simon & Schuster, Inc.

MARGARET K. McELDERRY BOOKS is a trademark of Simon & Schuster, Inc.

For information about special discounts for bulk purchases, please contact Simon & Schuster Special Sales at 1-866-506-1949 or business@simonandschuster.com.

The Simon & Schuster Speakers Bureau can bring authors to your live event. For more information or to book an event, contact the Simon & Schuster Speakers Bureau at 1-866-248-3049 or visit our website at www.simonspeakers.com.

Interior design by Rebecca Syracuse

The text for this book was set in Matrix II OT.

The illustrations for this book were rendered digitally.

Manufactured in the United States of America

0421 FFG

First Edition

2   4   6   8   10   9   7   5   3   1

Library of Congress Cataloging-in-Publication Data

Names: Weetman, Nova, author.

Title: It all begins with jelly beans / Nova Weetman.

Description: First edition. | New York : Margaret K. McElderry Books, [2021] | Audience: Ages 8–12. | Audience: Grades 4–6. | Summary: When they are selected to read speeches at their elementary school graduation, an unlikely friendship develops between two sixth-graders, one popular and one a misfit, who are facing family problems and health issues.

Identifiers: LCCN 2021004592 (print) | LCCN 2021004593 (ebook) | ISBN 9781534494312 (hardcover) | ISBN 9781534494336 (ebook)

Subjects: CYAC: Friendship—Fiction. | Schools—Fiction. | Mothers and daughters—Fiction. | Diabetes—Fiction. | Panic attacks—Fiction.

Classification: LCC PZ7.1.W429 It 2021 (print) | LCC PZ7.1.W429 (ebook) | DDC [Fic]—dc23

LC record available at https://lccn.loc.gov/2021004592

LC ebook record available at https://lccn.loc.gov/2021004593

For Emily Gale, who always shares her jelly beans

Chapter 1

MEG

MY CURRENT BEST FRIEND IS a brown paper bag that has a slight crease in the corner. I take it everywhere. This particular bag has been with me for about two months now, although it's getting ratty along the edges, so it won't hold my air for much longer.

I stash my old bags in a drawer in my room because I can't bring myself to throw them out. After I hide the old one, I go hunting for a plain, recycled, thick paper bag that will withstand the force of my lungs blowing into it. Bags like that are harder to find than you might think. Mushroom bags are good, or bags that have held fancy loaves of bread. I tried naming my bags at the beginning, but it felt a bit sad, so now they're just the Bag.

I didn't always have the Bag for a friend. I used to have a real best friend. Her name was Eleanora. I was so impressed that someone with such a sophisticated name was my friend, I'd say her full name as often as I could. She had four syllables. I only have one. Meg. Actually, that's not true. It's Margaret, which I like even less than Meg. It's as dull as my mousy brown hair.

Eleanora isn't around anymore. That makes it sound like she's dead. She's not. She just ditched me and made friends with other girls who don't carry paper bags in their pockets, leaving me here, in the nurse's office, with mine.

The nurse's office is a fluoro-lit room down the corridor from the principal's office, where the Bag and I sometimes spend part of the school day. At first my teachers tried to coax me back to their classrooms, although now they've accepted that I hang out here on occasion. Actually, if I were to fill in a questionnaire about how frequently I was in here, I'd probably lean toward the "Often" category. I like those questionnaires. I've filled in a few in the past year or so. There's something reassuring about seeing parts of your life broken down into a series of black marks in little boxes. It makes life feel more manageable.

The office lady, Sarah, who starts the day with red lipstick on her lips and ends the day with it smeared on her teeth, even sneaks me some leftover snacks from the staff room. It might be a piece of banana bread or a couple of cookies. The food makes me feel like I'm now one of the nurse's office's permanent residents, as regular as Dash Jones, the kid with asthma.

The nurse's office is about the size of a child's bedroom.

There's a single bed that nobody ever wants to lie on because it's hard to imagine the sheets are changed very often, and what if the kid who used it before you had stomach issues and vomited on the pillows? And there are a pair of armchairs that are too brightly covered in red-and-yellow patterned vinyl like they've been stolen from the children's hospital, where the furniture is all primary colored to lift the mood of the patients. The only wall decoration is a poster of a Healthy Eating Pyramid that is torn in one corner, and there's a straw basket of picture books left there for kindergarteners to read when they are having a bad day. When they built Bayview East Elementary School, they should have consulted the students to see how many of us might need to frequently use the nurse's office, because then they would have worked out that it needs to be much larger than it is. Although that is assuming, of course, that anyone cares about those of us spending time in here, and that is probably unlikely.

There's nothing pleasant about the room, although I still spend a lot of my time here. It's tricky to explain why. My friend the Bag knows why, although nobody else really does. Except for Sarah in the office, because she knows everything about everyone in this school, but she's never actually said anything directly to me.

The reason I walked out of class today is because it's Thursday, and on Thursdays we have an hour of PE and today we're running four laps of the track and I happen to be wearing slippers, and if I go to PE then my teacher will do two things:

first he will lecture me about wearing inappropriate footwear, and then he will make me run anyway in the inappropriate footwear.

I'd like to think that if I were a teacher, I'd guess that my wearing slippers to school wasn't through choice. And then maybe I'd actually investigate what else might be going on. My PE teacher isn't really one to ask questions, though. He's a whistle man. He enjoys creating sharp noises and making us sweat.

Unsurprisingly, I'm really not up to PE today, so instead I'm in here, in the nurse's office, perched on my favorite of the chairs in the corner near the fridge. Usually I bring my book and reread the passages I love, but I forgot it this morning.

From this spot I can see the corridor through the open door, so I know when someone's coming. Preparation is key to a quiet life, which is my daily ambition. I can also hear the hum of the fridge filling in time. For the past five minutes, I've been looking through the glass door of the fridge, reading the labels of the medicines. It's really the school's fault, because if they don't want anyone knowing what medicines kids are taking, they should keep them somewhere a bit more discreet.

I've now learned that Jacob in grade two is asthmatic, and Emily in grade four is anaphylactic if she comes into contact with chocolate, eggs, or strawberries. Poor Emily. I thought it was hard having *my* life. Removing chocolate and strawberries is something else altogether. One kid is on Ritalin for ADHD, and someone else requires oral steroids. I didn't bother investigating Dash's medication, because he told me all about it last year. It's like a miniature pharmacy in there.

"Hey," a voice says, and I turn my attention to the door as quickly as I can, trying to pretend that I'm not reading the labels after all.

It's Riley Jackson, another girl from grade six. She started at my school toward the end of last year, so I don't really know her. She doesn't look so good and I hope she's not about to vomit on me. That would make me wish I'd stayed in PE, and I never wish that. Riley's tall and skinny and her ponytail is slightly messier than usual. She's in shorts and a patterned T-shirt, and she's wearing the black-and-white fabric fanny pack she always wears around her waist. I've tried to find out about the fanny pack, but it makes it hard when I don't have anyone I can ask. She crashes in through the doorway and drops down on the bed. I jerk out of reach so we don't bump legs. Touching isn't really my thing.

"Riley, I'm calling your parents." Sarah bundles in after her.

I look away from them. This is one of those moments when I hate being in the nurse's office. Two kids are definitely enough to fill this space; two kids and a grown-up who is taller than most dads make it claustrophobic. I see Sarah look across at me and I clutch the Bag. It's a just-in-case clutch. The last thing I want is for Sarah to make me leave because Riley's medical needs trump mine. I have to stay here until PE is finished.

"No, I'm okay," says Riley as the office phone starts ringing.

"You sure?" says Sarah.

"Yeah. I'm fine. Really," she says in a voice that sounds anything but.

"I have to get that. I'll be back to check on you," Sarah says, rushing off.

I wonder if Sarah expected to be a full-time receptionist and a full-time nurse when she took this job. She is about my mother's age, or maybe even older. Her hair is silvery in threads at the front but the rest is brown.

"What are you in here for?" says Riley, looking over at me.

"Carjacking." I'm not about to tell her the truth.

She stabs a short laugh that's not entirely unfriendly and then stops, her face turning even whiter than when she came in.

"If you're going to vomit could you please direct it elsewhere?" I ask.

She gives me a strange look.

"You look rather pale," I tell her.

"Nah, it's nothing. Hey, I like your T-shirt."

I look down as if I'm trying to remember which one I'm wearing. Of course I know its Gumby, because it's always Gumby. I don't have any others, but that information is private.

"Is it old?"

"Age is all relative, isn't it?"

"What?"

She maneuvers her body so she's half sitting, half leaning back against the spotty-covered cushions. I notice her

Converse and wonder if she's spied my slippers. I tuck my feet back under the legs of the chair like somehow that will make my slippers disappear, but she's still peering at my feet. So I take a deep breath and scrunch my eyes as tight as I can and practice seeing blue water.

"What are you doing?" Riley asks.

"Relaxing," I tell her.

"Good luck with that."

I snap my eyes open. She's watching me as she pops a bright green jelly bean into her mouth. Where did that come from? Then I notice a small bag of colored jelly beans perched on her lap. My stomach flutters at the sight.

"You want one?"

Riley holds out the bag and I can see the tremor in her hand. I take too long to decide and she sighs, so I grab the brightest thing I can see: a fluorescent blue bean. Instead of eating it, I grip it, feeling the thick, sugary crust crush in my fist.

She eats another jelly bean and then tosses a pink one into the air and catches it in her mouth.

"You should probably hide them from Sarah," I say. "We aren't supposed to eat candy at school."

Riley laughs like I know nothing. Maybe she doesn't care about rules.

"Do I still look like I'm going to throw up?"

"A bit."

"Don't worry. I'm not." She sits forward. "This bed is all lumpy."

"That's the germy bed. Those in the know avoid it at all costs."

She looks down at the mattress. "Why?"

"Unsurprisingly, the sheets are rarely washed."

Riley laughs, and the sound is light. "To be honest, that makes me want to sit here even more!"

She wriggles to the edge of the bed and swings her Converse back and forth like she's on a ride in a theme park. "You going to eat that jelly bean or just play with it?"

I unpeel my fingers and peek at the blue bean. I bite it in half, pretending for a second that I can savor it, and then suddenly suck the whole thing into my mouth. It tastes like cheap grape jelly and my stomach rumbles for more.

"Here, have as many as you want. I have heaps in my locker," says Riley, throwing me the plastic ziplock bag.

I try to think of something smart to say, something that prevents her from knowing how much I want to eat the lot, though I can't. I'm rarely stuck for words and I wonder what it is about Riley that has caused this particular condition.

"Have you done another test, Riley?" asks Sarah, bustling back in.

I'm holding the candy in full view and I wonder for a second if it was Riley's intention that I get busted with them instead of her. I quickly wedge them between my back and the chair.

"I was just about to," she says, unzipping the long fanny pack from her hip and taking something out. I can't quite see what it is because Sarah's now blocking my view. What test would she be doing? What is wrong with her?

I hear a beep and then Riley says, "It's back up to four. I'm fine now."

"Good. But I want you to stay here for another ten minutes and then you can go back to class. Okay?"

"Sure. That means I get out of PE," Riley says lightly. A fellow PE dodger. Maybe we have more in common than I first thought.

While Sarah's looking the other way, I manage to pop a green jelly bean into my mouth. This one is a strange lime flavor. I'm not sure I like it.

Sarah leaves again and Riley sits up properly this time. She doesn't look white anymore.

I take a couple of jelly beans and pass the bag back. "Thank you," I say.

She shrugs and zips them into her fanny pack. I wait, expecting her to tell me what she was testing.

"So, what's wrong with you?" she says instead.

I don't really know how to answer, so I quote a line from my favorite book: "I'm in the depths of despair," I tell her.

She frowns at me and leans closer, peering at my face. "You're what?"

I shrug, having decided long ago that one of the only currencies I have is mystery.

"I thought this place was for sick people," she says, swinging her legs out of the bed.

"It's a public space, and despair is a medical condition," I say defensively.

"It's called the nurse's office and it's for *sick* people. Just saying. I'm going to PE now. If Sarah comes back, tell her I left."

She pushes past me, her hip banging into my elbow. When she reaches the doorway, she swivels and stares at me for a second, taking in my slippers again, and I can feel the stickiness of the jelly beans on my teeth. Then she walks off down the corridor and she's gone, and I'm back to the hum of the fridge, reading the labels on the medicines and hanging with my friend the Bag.

Chapter 2

RILEY

STARTING THE SCHOOL WEEK WITH a conversation about how apparently Nick Zarro has a crush on me is not my idea of fun. I don't believe it for a second but my friends have been giggling and writing me notes about it. I most definitely do not think I like Nick. He's much too sure of himself, and when he talks to me he always looks past me like I'm not very interesting. I'm pretty sure I'm more interesting than him. In fact, I'm pretty sure that even Meg's slippers are more interesting than him. But by far, his biggest mistake was when I first started at this school, and he made a joke about my insulin pump and told me I looked pregnant because of the bag I wear around my stomach with my testing kit. I've never forgiven him for that. And even if he apologized a million times and bought me a really awesome present, I still don't think I ever would.

"He told Matt yesterday that he liked you," whispers Lina.

"Whatever." I resist the temptation to add an eye roll.

One of our teachers, Mr. Sanderson, is midway through explaining BIDMAS to us and I really need to concentrate because I have no idea what he's talking about.

"Don't you like him even a bit?"

"No. Not one bit," I say louder than I intend.

"Riley Jackson? Do you want to come and explain this concept to the rest of the class?" Mr. Sanderson has that teacher stare happening. I look away first.

"Um, no, sorry."

I elbow Lina sharply, hoping she understands the physical code for *shut up*. She nudges me back and slides her notepad over. There's a line of gray sketchy love hearts that she's drawn as a border around the math equations. This time, I go all-out on the eye roll.

My friends at this school are always talking about boys. It's not that I don't like boys. I might. Or I might not. I'm just not even thinking about all that stuff yet.

Besides, if I was going to crush on someone, it wouldn't be Nick Zarro or the other boys in my class. That's what totally drives me mad about all these conversations. Apparently, if a boy likes me, I'm supposed to be so flattered that I have to like him back. It doesn't seem to matter what I actually think of him. I explained this to Lina but she just looked at me like I was an alien and then told me I should be happy if someone's crushing on me. Like I don't have better things to care about.

"Riley, can I see you for a second?" Ms. Barber, the year coordinator and my favorite of the grade six teaching team is standing in the door. I like her because she talks about gender and equality and cracks down hard on Matt Park and his friends who sometimes make really annoying jokes about the girls.

Mr. Sanderson sighs as I get up to leave. He thinks math is more important than pretty much anything else. I'd love to tell him the truth. That doing math is like eating broccoli—you know you have to do it but you want it over with as quickly as possible.

I follow Ms. Barber out to the teacher office. One desk is covered in confiscated Pokémon cards and another has several blocks of opened chocolate on it. There are notes scribbled in handwriting messier than mine stuck to the walls. I try to read them, but Ms. Barber turns her head around to face me.

"Mrs. Myer would like you to make one of the speeches at graduation," she says.

Mrs. Myer is the principal and we haven't had much to do with each other. I've noticed she wears a lot of brown and her hair rarely moves, but I've never actually talked to her. I frown, suspicious. "Why me?"

Ms. Barber smiles. "You're a good student. You're a good leader and you're . . . you're . . ."

"Different?"

"We're all different," says Ms. Barber, trying to catch my eye.

I can't help but smirk at her. Graduation is five and a half weeks away. But apparently it's a huge deal at this school.

There's a dinner and an after-party dance in the gym and everyone gets all dressed up. I hope they spray the gym with something so that it doesn't smell like sweat and sneakers. My friends have been talking about it for ages. It sounded like fun, until I was chosen to make some sort of silly speech in front of everyone. We both know the reason I'm being asked. Even though I've only been here for a year I've already worked out that Mrs. Myer likes to show off anything different about her school, like somehow it reflects better on her. It might be the playground, it might be the art class, or it might be the new kid.

"Don't be too cynical, Riley. You're one of our strongest students."

When I started at this school at the end of last year, after we moved down from Sydney for Dad's work, it was Ms. Barber who checked in every few weeks to make sure I was okay. She was the teacher who did diabetes training so I could go on field trips without Mum freaking out. For weeks, until I became friends with Lina and the others, I would hang out with Ms. Barber at lunchtime and talk about cats. Hers is called Lizard, because he slinks around and lies in the sunniest spots in the backyard, soaking up the warmth. We used to have a cat called Jelly but she stayed in Sydney with Granny, because she said if we were all abandoning her, the least we could do was leave her the cat.

"Sorry," I tell her.

"It's a big deal."

"Okay . . ." I force a smile, making an effort because I like her.

"And how are you feeling about graduating? About junior high?"

I pretend to think, when actually I don't know the answer. "Fine. Excited."

Ms. Barber nods and I notice the second piercing in her ear, the flash of green when she moves her head. "Transitioning to junior high can seem pretty overwhelming."

"I've moved states *and* schools. It'll be fine." But even to me, this sounds like a lie. Leaving Sydney was horrible.

I've been trying *not* to think about finishing elementary school, because my friends aren't coming with me. I'm going to the local school. My friends are going to private schools. Lina's been desperate to talk Mum into sending me to the same school as her, but there is no way my parents will go private. They both went to public schools and they think they turned out okay. It's one of the rare things they agree on, other than my regular bedtime and the amount of carbohydrates in a banana.

I also know that starting at a new school again means more explanations about diabetes and the fanny pack I wear to carry the black insulin pump with a plastic line connecting to my stomach. Some people suggest the stupidest theories. Like, it's because I'm a robot. Yep. Thanks Matt Park. Hilarious. Or another favorite is that it's my spy phone. That was Jackson Something in grade four at my old school. As if. Isabelle Doherty used to joke with her friends that it was an illegal listening device and they should all stay away from me. Joy. It also means I sometimes get treated differently. I hate that the most.

I try to hide my pump inside the fanny pack, but it can be hard, especially if I'm wearing fitted clothes or if I have to take out my pump to put in carbohydrates.

A new school also means finding somewhere private to do a test, that isn't the bathroom. I've never liked hiding out in a smelly stall to do a test.

Before Ms. Barber can grill me any longer, there's a little knock on the glass, and I see Meg hovering.

"Come in, Meg," Ms. Barber says warmly.

Meg stares at me as she shuffles into the room and sits next to Ms. Barber. Until we spoke to each other in the nurse's office last week, we'd never had a conversation. I don't know her deal but there are plenty of rumors about how poor she is, and how strange. She's wearing the Gumby T-shirt again so maybe it's the only one she has. To be honest, it sort of annoyed me that she was in the nurse's office when she didn't need to be. It's not like *I* have a choice.

"Meg, Mrs. Myer has requested that you make a graduation speech at the ceremony," says Ms. Barber.

From the look on Meg's face, I'd say she's even more suspicious about this whole thing than I am.

"Sorry, but I don't like the sound of that," says Meg.

"You'll be fine. I'll be right there with you," Ms. Barber says gently.

Meg holds up a wrinkled brown paper bag and shakes it at Ms. Barber. "I can't."

Now I'm intrigued. What's in the bag?

"I'll help you," says Ms. Barber quietly.

"I'm not going to graduation anyway," Meg says clearly.

"Why not?"

"It's just a chance to wear a dress and brag about yourself," Meg tells Ms. Barber.

I smile a little, trying to hide it behind my hand, but I sort of agree.

"Whoa! Why don't you tell me what you really think?" says Ms. Barber.

I don't actually think Ms. Barber minds Meg's honesty. She's one of those teachers you can say anything to. I like the way she tries to catch Meg's eye, before saying, "You don't have to come. But you do have to write a speech. You're the best writer in grade six. Mrs. Myer wants a diverse spread of students. Blow us away; I know you can," she says.

Meg looks at me and takes a noisy breath and I'd love to know what's she thinking.

"Okay, well, you two will have to meet with Mrs. Myer at some point. She hasn't chosen the boys yet, but she will."

The lunch bell rings, and instantly there is noise around us. Meg scurries off and I spy her slippers again. Who wears slippers to school? I imagine Mum's face if I tried to sneak out of the house wearing mine. Who am I kidding? The chance of me ever sneaking out of the house, with or without slippers, is about a billion to one.

"If you have any questions, just come and find me, Riley," says Ms. Barber.

I head out of the office into the rush. Everyone's stampeding to put away their books and their folders and grab their lunch boxes. Today I'm slow. Swallowed up in the hurry.

"Look!" Lina bops up in front of me, holding a bunch of pale mint-green envelopes in front of my face. She's beaming. I know what they are. It's not like she's been talking about anything else for the last two weeks.

"Awesome! I love the color."

"Yeah, me too. I was going to choose blue," she says.

"To be honest, green is much nicer," I tell her.

"It's mint, not green. Come on," she says, grabbing my arm.

"Bathroom," I tell her, lying. "I'll meet you out there."

She pulls a face, but then notices Elle and Tessa heading outside. "Whatevs," she says, impatient to catch up with our other friends.

I'm supposed to check my blood glucose levels before I eat, like every time. And I sort of haven't been lately. But after ending up in the nurse's office last week I'm trying to be more careful, because Mum's lectures are next level. I'd rather wait and do it alone in the empty common room than outside where everyone eats lunch and can see.

I'm diabetic, if you didn't already know that. I have an insulin pump that goes straight into my stomach, which I've had since I was in grade four. If I didn't have the pump, then I'd have to inject insulin into myself, which I'd hate, particularly at school. I have to calculate the grams of carbohydrates for the food I eat and then put them into the insulin pump and then the pump releases the insulin for me.

To be honest—or TBH, as I like to say—I sort of think it's only my fingers and my stomach that are diabetic. The rest of me is pretty normal. I'm not supposed to use that word. Mum always corrects me when I do. Tells me there's no such thing as normal and it's just a construct and yada yada yada. I tune out when she goes into psych speech. She's a psychologist so there's a lot of that sort of talk. Secretly, I call her the Brain.

I know she's right. But what she doesn't get is that I don't feel normal or abnormal. I know there's nothing wrong with me, and I know being the same as everyone else does not make you "normal," but the only parts of me that are directly injected or pricked are my fingers and my tummy. So, I think of myself in two halves—the body bits that are tested and the body bits that aren't. I haven't tried to explain that to Mum. I'm sure she'd think it was stupid, but it makes sense to me.

I turn away from the few kids who are still riffling around in their lockers and prick my finger. I feel how hard the end of the skin is from where it's been jabbed thousands of times. I like the toughness of the skin. I squeeze the tip and a perfect red bead pops out. I insert the strip into the meter and then add a small drop of blood to the end of the testing strip. There's a beep and the number 5.2 is displayed. My blood glucose level is within the range it should be. Mum will be happy.

When I look up, I see Meg watching me from the other side

of the room. She's fully staring, which is sort of creepy because nobody else is in here.

"You good, Slipper Girl?" I call out. I hate being watched while I do a test.

My words must break the spell because she spins around and hurries off. Maybe she's heading to the nurse's office, even though she's not even sick. I can't believe anyone would want to hang out in there if they didn't have to.

Chapter 3

MEG

USUALLY I GO SHOPPING AFTER school on Wednesdays because that's when Mum has money, so it means that lunches on the two days before I shop are even smaller than usual. Today I had a squashy tomato and a cracker, and now, thanks to Sarah, I'm working my way through the leftover cheese and biscuits from the teachers' morning tea. The door to the nurse's office bangs open. I was hoping for a quiet hour or two, but apparently, I have company. I don't like sharing the nurse's office when I'm eating the teachers' scraps.

"Afternoon, Meg," says Dash, another resident.

I snatch up the last biscuit from the plate. Dash is wearing his daily uniform of choice. A pair of blue cotton shorts and one of the many Star Wars T-shirts he seems to own.

"Hi, Dash," he says to himself. "You're looking lovely today.

Why thank you, Meg. I washed my hair last night. And it has to be said that you're looking lovely as well."

I keep breathing. In and out, pretending the Bag is over my mouth.

"It's just me, Meg. You don't have to breathe like that. Remember."

"Don't you have a class to go to?" I snap as he squeezes past me. I haven't even had a chance to chat with Sarah like I normally do.

"She speaks!" Then he sighs and perches on the edge of the bed. "Cross-country training."

"My deepest condolences."

Dash smiles at my understanding, and I see a flash of colored braces lining his teeth. He hates PE almost as much as I do. Not for the same reasons as me, rather because he claims he has better things to do than throw a ball back and forth. I suspect it's also because of his asthma. Dash isn't like the other asthma kids who can do most things as long as they have their inhaler nearby. His asthma is severe. It makes him wheeze and cough and frequently head off to hospital. He's in grade five, although he seems older. He spent most of grade one in hospital reading the Lord of the Rings series, and most of grade two rereading it. He explained he knows things because he has a bunch of older teenage girl cousins and an older sister, Elle, and they forget he's younger. I think he's just observant, like most kids who've had to sit out of things and watch the world go on around them.

Like me, he's short, although, unlike me, he has heaps of friends. Sometimes they even accompany him to the nurse's office and hang out until he's feeling better. If I'm in attendance when they try that, though, I quickly send them on their way. This place isn't built for friendly helpers. As far as the nurse's office companions go, he's one of the better ones. Except when I feel like being alone.

"Explain to me why we are made to run three miles in a circle," he says.

I shake my head. I'm the wrong person to ask.

"Pointless," he says. "Mum bought me these new sneakers for it. What do you think?"

He holds his feet out and we both look down. They are black with a blue stripe down the sides. Then he must notice my slippers, because his head jerks up. Obviously his sister hasn't told him yet about my latest fashion choice.

"Oh, Meg, I'm sorry. They're just stupid shoes."

"Well they look like quality," I tell him.

He nods and his cheeks are slightly red. I know he's embarrassed because he's just shown off his new sneakers while I'm sitting here in slippers. If it were anyone else, I'd delight in their embarrassment. Dash fixes his hair, like he's trying to think of what to say. It's not like him to be stuck for words.

"Yeah. It's the stripe. Supercharges you," he says finally, looking up at me with a tentative smile.

"Tell me, Dash, have you ever come across Riley Jackson in the nurse's office before?" I ask him.

"Who's Riley Jackson?"

I roll my eyes at him and he laughs. He's also a resident jokester.

"Let's see," says Dash, preparing to give me the rundown. "Riley Jackson. Plays netball in Elle's team. She looked promising for a few months but now seems to have joined the dark side. They even have the same hairstyle. But you already know that. According to Elle, her parents are super strict, so she doesn't hang out at our place with the others. Instead, I'm frequently stuck with Lina. And even our dog disappears when Lina's around," he says with a groan.

"Riley didn't get my *Anne of Green Gables* quote," I say, feeling mildly disappointed.

He laughs. "Nobody gets your quotes. Stop pretending you don't like it that way!"

He's right. I like quoting characters and knowing most people my age have no idea what I'm talking about. It's rare for me to feel superior, so I take any chance that I get.

"And, Meg . . . we're talking about one of Lina's friends. Remember how much Elle changed when she started hanging out with her? Lina's like an amoeba: expanding every second, sucking up everyone around her so she can feed on them," he says, like that should be enough to make me stay away. And it should.

Lina Surfy's one of those girls I've spent my life avoiding. Even before Dad died and things changed at home, I instinctively knew to stay away. Dash has never liked her much, either. She's mean enough to kids her own age. She's brutal to anyone younger.

"I wasn't asking about Riley because I want to be her friend. She came into the nurse's office the other day. I was wondering if you knew why."

He shrugs. "No idea. I can find out, though."

I don't want Dash to spy for me. "No thanks."

He leans down to grab a book from the colored straw basket near my feet.

"What are you doing?"

"I'm trying to be helpful," he says, holding up a picture book called *Duckling Disaster* with a tatty cover of a duckling peering over the top of a bluestone wall.

"Once upon a time . . . ," he starts to read.

"No."

"But you love this one," he says.

I narrow my eyes at him and glare up from behind my fringe. "No."

"It's the one where the duckling loses her sister down the well."

"No."

He dramatically drops the book back into the basket.

"You ruin all my fun, Meg."

"I do my best," I say, kicking off my slippers and tucking one leg underneath me. And as I do, the Bag dislodges from where it's been wedged down the side of the chair and flutters down onto the floor.

Dash reaches it first and holds it out to me. I don't look at him as I snatch it away, and as I do, I hear the rip as a small piece of brown paper tears at the top.

"Sorry, Meg, I didn't mean to . . ."

I check the damage and it's only small, but still, soon I'm going to have to start looking for a new one.

"Here's the scrap, I'm sure we can fix it," he says. "I'm good with a glue stick."

I roll my eyes, though a tiny smile sneaks out too. Only Dash could get away with this. He smiles back, takes the Bag off me, and throws it up into the air. We both watch as it floats gently down and sails underneath the germy bed.

Chapter 4

RILEY

MY FRIENDS ARE HANGING OUT under the square monkey bars near the fence. There are three of them. I make four. Our posse. When I started here it took a while to find friends, partly because I knew it meant I had to explain diabetes and that's hard sometimes. Then one day during PE, Lina chose me for her team because we were wearing matching pastel cat T-shirts and that was that.

"Finally!" Lina says, holding up the green envelopes. "You took ages, R!"

There's no point explaining that I was doing a test. They are like goldfish with their tiny memories.

"Party invite time!" Tessa says, clapping her hands together.

Elle moves across so there's space for me between them.

"Mum had them printed at work," Lina says as she hands out the envelopes. Our names are in flowing black print across the front. It sort of looks more like a wedding invite than one for a kid's birthday, but I know better than to say that aloud.

Tessa starts to tear hers open, but I shake my head at her, knowing it will unravel Lina if we ruin the envelope. I tuck my finger under the back and slide gently along the seal, popping it open. Then we all take out our invites together.

The invites have magnets on the back so they can be stuck straight onto a fridge. On the front, there's a picture of Lina beaming in the middle of me, Tessa, and Elle on Athletics Day last term. I know why Lina used an old photo. She has braces now, and nobody is allowed to take her picture again until they come off. If you looked up "vain" in the dictionary, there's a good chance Lina would be the definition.

"It's at a hotel!" Elle squeals, reading ahead.

"No way!" Tessa says as she holds up the invite and a sprinkle of fairy dust flutters down over her lap and into the dirt.

"Cool," I manage, pretending to be engrossed in reading. It's not that I'm not excited about Lina's party; it's just that it's complicated. And my friends don't understand how complicated.

Lina giggles and starts to explain the party. "It's only three weeks away."

She pulls her phone out from her lunch box and shows Tessa and Elle photos of the pool, while I sit back and watch.

My old friends in Sydney would never have had a pool party at a hotel. They were into playing sports and fighting the boys for their right to use the track at lunch. My new friends are different. They are all about clothes and hair and matching pencil cases. Lina has brown eyes, shaggy, long blond hair, and perfectly manicured nails. She's been doing gymnastics since she was two and is always showing off. Tessa and Elle could be sisters. They're both dark-haired and they wear shorts and stripy T-shirts. And the three of them always have their denim jackets tied around their waists.

"Just look at the size of the beds!" Lina tells me, holding the phone up to my face. I scroll through the photos. It all looks very glamorous.

"It's going to be great," I tell her.

"I'm going to see if my mum will let me do something like that too," says Tessa.

"Me too," says Elle.

Lina laughs. "That's an awesome idea. Let's all have our sleepover birthday parties in hotels in the city. We'll be like the hotel sleepover club."

I tune out while Tessa, Elle, and Lina make plans that I doubt will involve me. Lina grabs my arm, her orange-painted nails flicks of foreign color on my pale skin.

"You can come, R, can't you?"

"Yeah, course. As if I'd miss it."

She sighs, dramatically relieved. "Just had a thought that maybe your mum might not let you . . . you know . . ."

"She'll let me. It's your birthday!" I might have to get my sister, Jenna, to help me work on Mum. She's the expert in negotiation. And if that fails, then she just lies. To be honest, though, there's no way Mum will let me go. As if.

Lina beams at me. I smile back but start running scenarios through my head. Maybe I can suddenly get sick the night before the party. Something gross like a stomach bug. None of them would want to catch that. It worked the last time I was supposed to go into the city with them for an afternoon of shopping. One thing is for sure. I definitely can't tell them the truth: that Mum doesn't trust Lina's mum to look after me. That Mum doesn't trust me. I need to direct the conversation somewhere else. And fast.

"What's up with Meg?"

"Weirdo Meg?" Lina asks.

I can just imagine how Mum would react if she could hear this. She's already down on my friends, but this would seal it. I'd never be allowed to even talk to Lina again, let alone go to her birthday party.

"Yeah. She was in the nurse's office last Thursday, but she wasn't actually sick."

Tessa laughs, and it's a mean sound. "Sick in the head, maybe!"

"What's with the slippers, though?" I ask, knowing this is bound to reel them in.

"Is she wearing slippers to school?" Lina leans in, liking this bit of information.

"I haven't noticed." Elle shrugs. "I guess I don't pay that much attention to her."

Pleased we've moved away from the birthday party, I stretch out my legs and watch my friends eating their lunches.

"Yeah. Old ratty ones. I've dubbed her Slipper Girl," I say, feeling a flutter in my stomach. *Sorry, Meg,* I think, *but you're the perfect distraction.*

"Slipper Girl . . . I like it," says Lina, grinning at me. "Next time I see her, I'm going to call her that."

The flutter in my stomach just became a stampede.

"What did Barber want you for?" Lina asks. She abbreviates all the teachers to a last name only.

"She asked me to do a graduation speech."

"Not fair! I asked her if I could do one," Lina says sulkily.

I hadn't realized it was such a big deal. "You can write mine if you want. I don't want to do it," I say lightly.

"Who else is doing it?" Lina asks.

"Slipper Girl," I whisper, feeling slightly wobbly as I say it.

Lina's eyes widen and she starts shaking her head. "No. Way. She won't even go to graduation! Angry!"

Elle and Tess have slipped into silence. I've noticed it happens sometimes when Lina is talking. Lina sort of sucks up all the air and there's no room for anyone else to have an opinion.

"Seriously. Why would she choose her?" Lina's sharp brown eyes drill into my face like somehow it's all my fault.

"I don't know. Apparently she's a good writer," I say.

"No point being a good writer if you haven't got anything to say!"

Lina leans back against the tree, and I can tell she's thinking hard. Maybe I can ask Ms. Barber to let Lina do the speech instead of me.

31

"Look, R," says Lina. "Nick's looking over here."

I turn and stare across at the track. Kids are screaming and laughing and trying to play tag right through the middle of a game of soccer. A couple of teachers stand and chat on the edge, eating their sandwiches and making sure nobody gets hurt. It takes me a minute to see Nick. And when I do, I notice that he's not looking over here. He's not even facing our direction.

"No, he's not."

"You missed it!"

"Lina!"

She shrugs.

"TBH, I don't like him anyway," I tell her.

"He's cute. I like his freckles," says Tessa.

"Yeah, I'll say," says Lina. "Really cute. You should go to 7-Eleven with him."

Without thinking, I laugh. "What for?"

Lina looks hurt and it surprises me. "A Slurpee or something."

I laugh. "I don't think Slurpees are on the list of Mum-approved foods. She'd kill me if she found out I had one."

"Well, you have to get better at hiding things, Riley," she says coldly.

"If I'm going to have to lie about a Slurpee, I'd rather have one with you guys than with Nick Zarro!"

Lina shrugs like she thinks I'm being uncool, but I know the only reason she wants me to hang around Nick Zarro is because she likes his friend—Matt Park. I lean back against the base of the gum tree and take out my thermos from my lunch box. Matt

Park is one of those predictable boys. Cute floppy hair, can handle a soccer ball, and thinks if he smiles in a certain way then the world will love him. TBH I'd probably be more likely to help Lina hang with her crush if it wasn't him.

"Pumpkin and potato soup again?" Elle asks as I unscrew the lid.

"I'm hoping not, but we both know Mum is a creature of habit!" I make a dramatic gesture to lift the lid, unveiling the orange gloop. "Yummy," I say sarcastically. "Tessa, trade?"

She shrugs and holds up her sandwich. "It's cheese."

I grin and pass over the thermos. Tessa's mum is Italian and she makes these incredible cheese sandwiches with thick white chewy bread and soft sweet cheese. Tessa prefers my soup. And I prefer pretty much anyone's lunch to mine.

Every day Mum makes my lunch even though every day I offer to do my own. When she's finished making it, she writes down the grams for everything and slides the Post-it Note into my lunch box so I won't have to work anything out. Bit tricky, though, when my lunch changes from a cup of specially measured pumpkin and potato soup to a carbohydrate cheese-and-white-bread dream.

I should estimate grams for the cheese sandwich. I should be honest with Lina about her party. I should be able to test in front of my friends. Instead, I bite into the crust of the sandwich and listen to them chatter on and on about sleepovers, graduation dresses, and boys and almost feel like I'm one of them.

Chapter 5

MEG

IT'S TUESDAY AFTERNOON, SO I leave the Bag on my bed and carry my dirty clothes, and some of Mum's, to the laundromat a few blocks away. We do own a washing machine and clothes dryer, although they aren't exactly operational right now. Dad used to keep everything electrical working in the house, and once he was gone, if they broke they stayed broken.

A bit like Mum, really.

We could get someone to fix stuff, but we can't afford it. Still, at least we own the house. Dad bought it years ago with his first big carpentry job, long before the suburb became fancy.

The Lost Sock is not the closest laundromat to our house, although it is the nicest. It also has the best name and a mural of lonely single socks that is always being added to by the lady who runs it. She's the other reason I go there. She's my dad's younger sister by five years and she helps to start the machines without me having to put any coins in.

Like me, her real name is Margaret, and like me, she doesn't call herself that. I'm Meg and she's Peggy. I don't call her Aunty Peggy because she says it makes her feel old. Every few weeks she has different-colored hair. I like guessing what color it will be, but I'm usually wrong. This week I'm betting it's a straw yellow.

It's only a twenty-five-minute walk to the Lost Sock, although I have to pass about nine restaurants and cafés and the only things I've eaten today are three crackers and a brown banana. I have to be famished to eat a banana. Sarah offered me some cake, too, but it was coffee flavored and the smell alone was unpleasant. I don't often refuse food, particularly when my stomach is growling, but even I have to have standards sometimes.

I was wrong about Peggy's hair. Today it's bright electric blue, not straw yellow. Even through the window I can see how vibrant the color is. She's at the back counter folding white towels. Her T-shirt is black and long like a dress, and I wonder if it's something someone left behind. She's often dressed in found objects, and sometimes, if they're too small for her, I end up with them. That's how I scored my favorite faded Gumby T-shirt that I wear almost every day to school. Early on I was terrified that someone would approach me on the street and reclaim their long-lost T-shirt, but now the pattern is so faded that I doubt anyone would care.

Peggy looks up as the little bell rings announcing my arrival.

She has the same blue eyes that my dad had, and they are almost as bright as her new hair color; if she's staring at you, her eyes are like laser beams, boring deep inside your mind. I drop my backpack of laundry onto the floor.

"You're late, Meg," she says warmly.

"And you're blue."

She grins and rubs her fingers through her short hair, making it stick up even more. "Do you like it?"

I nod. "Yeah, I do."

"I'm thinking I might keep it for a bit."

I laugh. "You always say that. I give it a week or two, no more."

She smooths her hands across the top of the folded towels and bags up the pile, ready for collection.

"Number seven's free," she says, nodding at the row of washing machines.

Even though I'm the only one in here, most of the other machines are chugging away, cleaning clothes and heating up the room. The Lost Sock is always warm and slightly damp, even in the middle of winter. When I first started coming here after our machine stopped working, Peggy told me how happy she was that I stayed while my clothes turned and cleaned, because most people shove in their coins and wander off for a coffee.

I upend my backpack into number seven and wait for Peggy to come and sprinkle the good detergent over the top. She always saves me some and won't let me use the cheap stuff from the vending machine. She says it's been there since the last owner.

"Here, put this on so we can wash Gumby," she says, handing me a black top with a silver unicorn on it.

I dash out the back through the little shuttered door and swap tops. Peggy knows Gumby's my favorite T-shirt, although I make sure she doesn't know it's pretty much my only T-shirt. Pretending is a skill I take very seriously, and one I have spent years perfecting.

I toss Gumby at the lid of the machine, like I'm shooting a goal. It falls short and Peggy scoops it up and adds it in with the detergent, slamming the lid down after it. Within seconds the sound of water whooshing into the barrel starts and I place both hands on the lid, feeling the vibration.

"That top suits you," she says, tugging on my sleeve. "You should keep it. It's been here for ages. You can't always wear Gumby!"

I suspect that it's Peggy's way of politely giving me new things that fit and things that weren't bought years ago. Even though I'm short and seem to be taking my time in the growth department, most of my old clothes are pretty ratty-looking and it's not like Mum takes me shopping on a regular basis.

"Thanks."

Behind us the tumble dryers flip clothes back and forth; it's a strangely comforting sound.

"You hungry, Meg?"

I raise an eyebrow. We both know the answer to that.

I follow her to the back room, where the walls change decoration as fast as her hair color. This week she's stuck up posters for some band I've never heard of. She pours me a glass of fruit punch from the jug she makes up.

I sip it and smile. "'I love bright red drinks, don't you? They taste twice as good as any other color.'"

Peggy laughs, recognizing the quote. She gave me *Anne of Green Gables* for my tenth birthday and I've read it seventy-three times.

"Sweet or savory, Miss Anne?"

I pretend to think. "Sweet."

"Don't know why I ask. It's always the same answer," she says.

"Okay—savory, then."

She ignores me and places an old wooden board on the rickety table in the corner. She opens a paper bag and slides out a puffed-up Boston bun, covered in the brightest, whitest icing and coconut I've ever seen. My stomach rumbles at the sight and I almost have to hold my hand back to stop it from snatching the bun off the board.

"Did I ever tell you about when I worked in a bakery? I was just a bit older than you. At the end of the day if we hadn't sold all the buns, I'd get to lick all the icing off," she says, hacking into the end of the bun with a blunt knife. "Your dad always made me bring home a bun for him, too. He loved this stuff."

She gives up on the cutting and pulls a chunk off with her

hands, placing it on an orange-and-purple patterned plate. "There's butter in the dish if you want it."

I don't. I just want to lick the icing and then eat the bread as quickly as I can so she'll offer me more.

"Any movement on the kindred spirits front?"

With a mouthful of icing I shake my head, wondering which of the girls in my class would even know what a kindred spirit was. Riley surfaces in my thoughts for a second, and I wonder why. It's not like I can imagine inviting her home for afternoon tea and sharing all my secrets. The idea makes me reach for more bun.

"Sometimes it takes a while to find our people," Peggy says quietly. "That's why books are so helpful," she adds, smiling.

I watch as Peggy twirls her electric-blue fringe around her finger and then lets go. My hair is about as unremarkable as the rest of me. It's just brown. I've often wondered what it would be like to have hair as red as Anne with an *e*. Maybe my daily life would sparkle and shine.

"You're wearing slippers?"

Nothing escapes Peggy.

"They're comfortable." I avoid looking at her, though I can tell she's watching me.

"Unfortunately nobody leaves shoes in a laundromat . . . but I could take you shopping?"

I shake my head, desperate to say yes. With shoes that fit I could almost pretend I fit, too. "No. It's okay. But thanks."

Peggy has offered to take me shopping a couple of times

lately. Although it's better for my mum if she doesn't. I don't mind her giving me T-shirts that have been left behind, but Mum is funny about Peggy offering us money or trying to help out. Anything Peggy does has to be well disguised.

"How's your mum?"

I swallow before I answer. "She vacuumed yesterday. And tidied the house. That's positive, isn't it?"

I watch as Peggy stares at me for a second and I know that she doesn't quite believe me. Then she changes knives and cuts a couple of slices from the bun, adding them to my plate.

"Has she phoned that lady I told you about?"

"I don't think so." Peggy gave me a name for Mum last time I was here. It's a doctor she thought might be helpful.

"I could try to talk to her again, if you like?"

I know that Peggy is only trying to help, but Mum isn't up to visitors. The last time she tried it didn't go so well. Afterward Mum stayed in bed for a week.

I shake my head. "No. It's okay."

Peggy reaches for my hand, giving it a squeeze. "She loves you. You know that, don't you? Grief does strange things to people. She'll get there."

Peggy's the only adult around who knows about Mum's sadness. She remembers who Mum was before. How funny and silly she could be. How she was always cooking and gardening when Dad was still alive. I try to remember her like that, but each month it's getting harder because those memories feel so long ago.

The bun is so sweet that my mouth puckers as I dive into the next slice.

"When you finish that, there's leftover curry in the fridge," she says, licking stray icing from the ends of her fingers. "I made extra so you can take some home to your mum."

Peggy is always making us meals. She constantly pretends she's made too much of something like spaghetti sauce or lasagna and then parcels it up in plastic tubs so I can take it home and reheat it. I bet Riley's family sits down to a home-cooked meal every night and takes part in vigorous debate. She doesn't know what she's missing. Leftover lasagna in complete silence has its charms too.

Peggy puts down two cups of cold milk on the table. My cup is unchipped, though hers is missing a handle. On Tuesdays, we always drink punch first and then milk.

"Did you hand in your English essay?" She licks her milk moustache and stares at me over the rim.

"Of course. Ninety-five percent," I tell her.

"You should have got one hundred percent! That essay was amazing."

"I think you might be biased," I say, grinning.

She shrugs. "I know a good essay when I read one. Do you need to use the laptop tonight?"

I shake my head. "I just have to work on a speech for graduation, and I can do that with a pen," I say, rolling my eyes.

Peggy laughs. "We didn't 'graduate' from elementary school. We just finished!"

I drain the last of the cold milk, feeling the chill of it on my teeth. "I know. It's a strange new tradition."

"Does anyone fail to graduate?"

"I can think of plenty of kids who should," I tell her, frowning.

"Is there a dinner or a dance?"

"Both. It's supposed to be some grand function where all the girls wear frilly dresses and the boys wear suits and talk about how elementary school was the best time of their lives. I don't think so!"

The bell dings out front and Peggy stands up slowly. I wait for her to say something else, but she just pats my hand and leaves me to it.

I hear her say hello to a customer as I focus on wiping my finger across another slice of Boston Bun until all the icing piles up in a sticky lump. I jam the whole thing into my mouth and let it ooze around.

"Meg, your washing's finished," calls Peggy.

I clean up before I leave. The back room is so compact and neat that it doesn't feel right to leave anything out of place.

"Look at this," Peggy says as I walk into the front part of the laundromat. She holds up a wad of socks that have electro-cuted themselves together as they've tumbled around inside a huge metal barrel. She separates one sock and places it above her head. A whisper of blue hair floats up to it.

"Static," she says, and laughs.

I open washing machine number seven and pull out the lump of clothes. They smell like oranges.

"You okay?"

"Yes," I say, struggling to carry the pile to the dryer in one go. The dryer's still warm from the last load, and I lean into the barrel, wondering what it would feel like to tumble around with the clothes. I might even discover what happens to all the missing socks.

Chapter 6

RILEY

LINA DOESN'T WEAR TRAINING BRAS. She wears a real bra, with lace. Apparently her mum took her shopping and they bought three different floral patterns. She loves it when we can glimpse the strap through her T-shirt. It's not even like she really needs a bra, but she likes pretending she's more developed than everyone else in grade six.

"Try this one," says Mum, banging into the change room without knocking.

I cover my chest quickly with crossed arms.

"I've seen it all before, Riley."

It's Friday morning and it's teachers' convention so no school for me, which means no work for Mum. Mum decided it would be a good opportunity to tick off all the jobs we needed to do. With a different mum that could mean a fun shopping trip for a graduation dress. Instead, mine is buying me a sports bra.

And not just any sports bra, but a navy blue one that looks like it's been made to withstand a bomb going off. There's no lace or patterns; it's chunky and solid and like something she'd wear. I slip my arms through and fiddle with the clasp, but I can't fasten it properly. Mum's cold fingers skim against my back as they clip the sides together.

I chance a look at myself. Instead of seeing the bra, I just see the tape covering the cannula into my stomach and the pucker marks on my skin where my line has been injected over the past few weeks. I stretch my arm across my middle, wondering what it would feel like to have nothing attached to your body.

"Still too big," says Mum, tugging on the straps. She swings the door open without warning, exposing me to anyone walking down the corridor, and disappears again.

Kicking the door shut, I sit down on the chair and slip out my phone from the pocket of Jenna's hand-me-down denim jacket. Elle has texted about Lina's present. We're putting in money to buy her a Polaroid camera. It's supposed to be a surprise, but she's hinted at it often enough that I'm sure she knows it's coming. I start texting back, wishing I was shopping with Elle and Tessa instead of being here with Mum.

"This is the smallest size they have," says Mum, barging back in and flinging another option toward me. This one is gray.

"Can't I just get something less ugly?"

"You don't need a bra yet, honey. You have tiny breasts," says Mum. "At least a sports bra will be useful protection."

"Mum..."

"Riley, come on. Off your phone." She grabs at my phone and tosses it into her handbag.

"Mu-um!"

I didn't even get to press send on the complaint text I was writing. She thrusts the gray bra in my direction, not bothering to apologize.

"Can we at least look for dresses?" I slip my arms in, cover my front, and turn around so Mum can do up the back. Just because I have to put up with Mum prodding my diabetic stomach doesn't mean I want her seeing all of me.

"Haven't you got something you can wear?"

"Graduation's a big deal. Everyone else has been shopping for weeks," I tell her, using my best whiny voice. TBH I know that's not true, but sometimes playing "the only kid not doing something" card works. Although it makes me wonder if Meg is really going to boycott graduation or if she was just saying it to shock.

Mum steps behind me so she can see over my shoulder and into the mirror.

"Nice," she says, nodding like she's achieved something great.

"As if . . ."

She smooths down a strap across my shoulder and I slap her hand away. I'm surprised when she laughs.

"When did you get so big, Riley? You're almost as tall as me."

"Leave, Mum," I tell her, pushing her out the door so I

can change back into my training bra and T-shirt in private. Looking in the mirror, I fix my ponytail and scruff up my fringe so it's not so neat. Mum keeps telling me I need a haircut but I'm desperate to grow it even longer like Lina's. She can almost sit on hers when she straightens it. My sister and I always had short hair when we were little, thanks to Mum. She said it was to keep lice under control, but I think it was just so that she didn't have to brush the knots out every night. She lives for practical.

Mum hands me a small bag with the bra folded up inside when I come out of the changing room. I really wish I could dump it on the ground for someone else to take home.

"Can we go to that shop on the second floor that Jenna likes?" I say, using my most innocent voice.

Frowning, the Brain pushes her glasses back up her nose. I'm sure she thinks it makes her look more like a psychologist. Her glasses magnify her eyes so I can see the specks of brown in the blue.

"Not for graduation," she says.

"Please, Mum. We're just looking."

"I'm not buying something too adult. . . ."

When I was little, Mum taught my sister and me a trick— to count to five before we answered so that we wouldn't say something we regretted. Now I mostly use the trick when I'm talking to her.

One, two . . .

She hurries off and I skip numbers three and four and trail after her. I have to step quickly to catch her. She's always so busy. Even shopping on a Friday morning, she walks so fast I can hardly keep up.

Today is what Lina would call a "scoping day." Apparently, you're supposed to scope at least six times before you actually purchase. I'm not quite as into shopping as Lina is. Maybe because I always go with Mum and there's no chance of doughnut eating or makeup testing. But Lina and the others spend half their life shopping. While they shop, I invent reasons why I can't go with them. I doubt Meg shops much. She's worn the same T-shirt for weeks. Not to mention her slippers. Maybe her mum is even stricter than mine.

The shop Jenna likes is called Hidden and it plays the sort of music she tunes out to most nights. Mum pulls a face as soon as we step through the door, like she needs to let me know how much she hates the place. I decide to go left while she heads right.

Most of the dresses are super short. Some are also backless. I'm scanning for one I think Mum will at least let me try on, but to be honest there aren't many to choose from.

"This would suit you," says Mum, holding up a pantsuit.

I shake my head. "Ew, no."

"You don't have to wear a dress, Riley," says Mum. "This is the twenty-first century. Women wear pants," she says, holding up her leg as if to show me proof that she's a woman and she's wearing pants.

"I want to wear a dress."

"Not usually."

"I do, Mum."

"Really? Or is Lina wearing a dress?"

I focus on the rack in front and grab at material that's sparkly and not me at all but will do as a distraction.

"That's been our biggest seller," says a woman a bit older than Jenna, who appears from nowhere like a genie out of a bottle. She's wearing ripped denim jeans, a low-cut white top, and huge dangly earrings.

"Not our style," says Mum, plucking it from my hand and returning it to the rack.

The woman laughs like this a scene she knows well. "What are you looking for?"

"Something appropriate for a child," snaps Mum.

"Um . . . something for graduation," I mumble. *One, two, three . . .*

"Okay, follow me," she says, striding around the shop in her towering heels and plucking dresses from both sides.

"Change room three is empty. If you need other sizes, just call out," she tells me, hanging about thirty dresses in the change room and smiling at us both.

I'm tired already.

Mum hustles in behind me and pulls the curtain across so hard, it comes loose at the other end.

"There's not much room, Mum," I tell her, wishing that for once I could get changed without company.

"It's fine."

Sighing, I turn away from her and start to undress.

The car ride to the hospital is silent. Not even music blares to fill in all the gaps between us. The only sound is from me biting chunks out of a green apple that Mum handed me when I complained I was hungry. She always has emergency apples in her bag, like there's a magic tree in there growing them.

"Did you do a test?" she asks.

"Yep."

"Fourteen grams," she says.

"Did it."

Mum stops at the lights and looks across at me. I concentrate on trying to shred the green skin with my teeth.

"The blue dress looked nice, but it wasn't amazing . . . ," she says.

"Uh-huh."

"I think we can do better."

I tried to tell her that the blue dress was perfect. It had a pocket for my test kit and pump so I wouldn't need my fanny pack. It didn't pull too tightly across my stomach so you couldn't see the infusion set. And it made me look like everyone else. But I can't say all that to Mum because she's forgotten what it's like being twelve.

"Not getting any greener, Mum," I say, nodding my head to the traffic lights.

She looks out the windshield and stops inspecting me with her well-practiced psych gaze.

Mum drives the car into the hospital car park and keeps circling down until it reaches basement level three. Mum always parks here. It's like she believes we're important enough to have our own allocated spot. I drop half the apple on the floor.

"Riley, you've put in fourteen grams; you have to finish the apple," she says, like I'm new to this diabetes thing. "I hope you don't do that at school. Although it would explain your low last week."

The apple's covered in floor fluff. I don't want to eat any more but I take a bite because arguing with her is even worse. It tastes weird.

Today I'm seeing Eda—my endocrinologist. I call her the Hulk. Nobody knows that, of course. Just me. It's not because she's green or even angry, but something about the quick way she shifts from friendly to serious reminds me of the Marvel character. I don't mind these appointments. I like the Hulk. I see her once every two months if everything is going okay.

"I'm going to get a coffee before we go up," says Mum, pressing the ground-floor button in the lift.

I follow Mum to the only café she believes makes a decent brew, and wait while she orders and hands over the glass travel mug she keeps in her bag so she can save the environment one takeaway coffee at a time. A display case of pre-prepared sandwiches, custard-filled cakes, and biscuits taunts me. The apple did nothing to fill the rumble in my stomach.

"Can I get a toasted sandwich?" I ask.

She shakes her head like it's a joke question not worthy of a real answer.

"I'm hungry, Mum."

"You had lunch two hours ago," she says. "And you just ate an apple. Or three quarters of one."

I notice her catch another woman's eye, and they share a look.

"Mum, two hours is a long time when you're young."

"Well, you'll have to wait." She fiddles with her plastic lid, attaching it to the top of the cup, and trots off toward the lift.

"Can you hear my stomach?" I say, running after her.

Mum laughs. "You'll live."

"Yeah, but you do realize you're starving me, and that's a matter for Child Services."

The doors open and I leap into the lift, pressing the button before she can.

"I'm going to tell Dad you've stopped feeding me."

"Riley . . ." Mum has this way of capping a moment so tight, you know if you shake it up further it will become a bubbling volcanic mess.

"Hungry," I say under my breath.

The lift dings and the doors open before Mum can hiss a reply. I leave her to chat nicely with the receptionist while I head through to the waiting area and take up residence in a spinny chair near the window. I can't see Mum from here, which means she can't see me, either. And that's the way I like it. This place looks pretty much the same as the hospital in Sydney. Electric-blue walls with oversized goofy animals painted on them, and furniture that is almost comfortable. The television is on. It's some kids' show with lumpy creatures dancing around in onesies. I watch it anyway.

Another kid lopes in. He's pretty young, maybe five or six years old. I've seen him before but I don't know his name. Even though endocrinologists don't just look after people with diabetes, the hospital schedules all the visits for certain conditions on the same day of the week. Friday is diabetes day so all the kids in today will have diabetes. Endocrinologists treat anyone who has a condition relating to their endocrine system, which controls hormones. My wacky hormone is insulin. The kids who come here on other days will have issues with their growth hormones or with their thyroid, or some other part of the endocrine system.

"Riley," says a voice.

I look around toward the corridor that leads to all the private rooms and see Eda with her sharp black fringe and glasses like Mum's that scream *I'm a doctor*.

"Hi," I say, jumping up and heading over. I reach Eda and realize that for the first time I'm exactly the same height as her. I must have grown without noticing. I can't see Mum anywhere and I'm hoping I can start the appointment before she realizes where I am.

"How are you?"

I shrug, knowing Eda will understand the response.

"Where's your mum?"

"Chatting, but we can start without her," I say lightly.

As Eda walks, I see the hint of a sly smile. She's tried in the past to have meetings with me that don't include Mum but they've been quickly shut down. "I'm sure she'll find us."

I follow Eda into her usual room. I've never been in here without a parent. It feels dangerous. Like I could spill all sorts of secrets and Mum wouldn't know.

I lean back in the slightly more comfortable chair than the one in the waiting room. The wallpaper in here is green with monkeys hanging from branches, like somehow that will trick us into loving our medical conditions and expressing our feelings.

At these visits, Eda looks at my average blood sugar levels (BGL) for the past three months (called an HBA1C blood test, or A1C for short) and my pump upload for the past week. Usually Mum would be interpreting the numbers for her like Eda didn't spend twelve years at university. Sometimes I think Mum's jealous because she only spent nine.

"How are you?" This time the question seems to hold more meaning. Eda looks at me over the top of her glasses.

I shrug. "Fine."

"Last time you were here we talked a bit about puberty. Did you read the pamphlets I gave you?"

I swallow, now wishing Mum would make an appearance. "Um . . . yeah."

Eda leans back in her chair. "Puberty starts with the release of estrogen for girls. And estrogen can cause insulin resistance so your body doesn't absorb insulin as well. This can have an added effect of higher blood sugar. You'll also be growing and filling out, so you need to eat more. That means more insulin."

I force a small nod, trying to look at Eda but feeling my cheeks starting to heat up. Talking about puberty with an adult is about the worst.

"Riley, your levels have been a bit less consistent lately," Eda says.

"Have they?" I ask, as if I don't know.

"Mmm. You had a low last week? And a couple of highs in the past month."

"Maybe." I think back to the nurse's office and how close I came to vomiting on the carpet right near Meg's slippered feet.

"The pump upload is showing that you're not testing enough at school. You need to be testing every time you eat, even if it's just a snack. I'm also aware that you're probably sharing food with friends. Right?"

I look up at her, waiting to see what she's going to say. The thing is it's fine most of the time, except when I forget to do a reading before I eat, or if I overcalculate or undercalculate the grams of carbohydrates, or deliberately forget altogether. Then it's not fine. Then I'll either have a high or a low, and if I have a low I have to treat it with jelly beans. And Mum lectures me. That's why I occasionally end up in the nurse's office. I also might have a low or a high depending on what I've eaten and if I've exercised or drunk enough water, or if I'm sick. Sometimes I feel low at netball and Mum makes me leave the court. There are tons of things that can throw off my readings, not just food. I wish I could say all that to Eda, but of course she's heard everything before.

She pushes her glasses back on her nose and continues.

"Riley, you need to learn how to estimate grams more accurately. I want you to come back and see the dietician. She can go through all of that."

I've been warned before that the pump upload is like Big Brother. Basically, there's nowhere to hide. It lets the Hulk see every interaction with the pump, or *lack* of interaction. I'm so lucky the Brain isn't in the room. She'd be yelling *I told you so.* She's always on me about testing before meals, and about sharing food. The thing is, I know I have to test. It's been drilled into me forever. I just don't always do it. Like I don't always eat my broccoli, or clean my teeth as well as I should, or wash under my armpits.

"Has something changed at school?" Eda asks.

"No. It's just . . ."

"Hard. I know," she says. "But this is an important time. It's your body, Riley. You need to take ownership over it."

"I want to . . ." *But Mum won't let me.*

At that exact moment, Mum bursts into the room looking flustered and concerned. I have to work hard not to smile at the sight.

"Have you started without me? Why didn't you come and get me, Riley?"

"It's okay, Tina, we're just having a chat."

Mum pulls out the chair next to me and sits down, sending me one of her special looks that she saves just for me and my *condition*.

"We're just talking about puberty and what that means for Riley's diabetes," says Eda.

"I've been studying the printouts and I'm concerned that her levels have been all over the place lately."

"Not really all over the place, Tina. And we've covered that. Riley's promised she'll do more testing at school," says Eda, holding Mum's stare. "Haven't you, Riley?"

"Definitely."

"It's her friendship group. It wasn't like this in Sydney," says Mum. "She's embarrassed to test in front of them."

"Mum," I say. "That's not true." It's not embarrassment. It's something else. My friends don't really understand how often I'm supposed to do a test. Like every time before I eat a meal. They think it's a part-time kind of condition, one that should fit in with my life. Not the other way around. Sometimes, if I do a test in front of them, one of them might want to help, which means they want to prick and squeeze my finger so a drop of blood bubbles up. They also love sticking the strip into the meter and waiting for the beep. I really hate it when they want to tell me the reading too, like I'm their patient.

"Actually, it's really common around this age for diabetics

to want their lives to be more like their friends. I think we can work together on this," says Eda, shooting me a reassuring smile.

"She needs to take her condition seriously," adds Mum.

On the inside I'm glaring at her because she's talking about me while I'm sitting right next to her, and I hate that. It's not hers to talk about. It's mine. My body, my diabetes, my *condition*.

"I'm sure she does," says Eda. "But I think it would help if Riley started meeting with the nurse and with me on her own. She needs to understand her body more so that she can look after it."

I want to cheer Eda for saying that. It's exactly what I've been trying to tell Mum for the past few months.

Of course, Mum snorts as if the idea is ridiculous. She doesn't actually argue with Eda but I know she's simmering away because she's chewing her lip like she's biting down all the bad things she wants to say.

I've only been seeing Eda for a bit over a year, but I feel like she's on my side and she always answers me first. Sometimes she even calls my parents "Mum" and "Dad" instead of Tina and Marcus and I know it drives them mad. But I like it. It's her way of telling them they are only here because I am.

"Shoes off, Riley," says Eda.

I've actually already unlaced my Converse because I'm one step ahead of her. I consider handing them to Mum, knowing that will make her even madder, but then I kick them under the table and stand up. I hate being weighed. Mum always follows us out to the scales and peers over my shoulder at the number to make sure I'm still within her narrow band of healthy.

As Mum stands up, Eda shakes her head. "We can handle it today, Tina. Come on, Riley, let's see how much you've grown," she says, leading me out to the corridor where the large metal scales wait.

As I reach the door I look back at Mum and watch as she sits back down, brushing unseen fluff from her shoulder.

Chapter 7

MEG

MUM DIDN'T MAKE IT OUT of bed for dinner last night, so I sat in the backyard with my book, a carrot, and a tomato sandwich and read until the light disappeared, forcing me back inside.

I checked in on her a couple of times. She had a headache that she said felt like her head was being split open. I refilled her glass of water and tried to find some painkillers in the medicine cupboard. All I found was an old packet of Dad's heart medication tablets that he used to take every day to lower his cholesterol. They didn't stop him from having a heart attack, though. His name had started to fade from the label, so I threw the packet out because I didn't want to see him vanishing.

Now I'm standing in my bedroom, getting dressed for school in my Gumby T-shirt and slippers. Every morning before

I leave for school, I smooth the sheets and plump the pillow and make my bed the way Dad used to. My room's just big enough for the single bed Dad built when I was three, an old white wardrobe covered in stickers, and a desk that functions as a dumping ground for the few things I own. I have a photo of Dad and me, taken on the day he taught me to ride a bike, and one of Eleanora and me in a school parade. My favorite photo is of Dad standing on the front step with his arm slung around Mum's shoulders and me squashed between them, beaming.

I see a flash of Dad. His hands that seemed as big as plates. His smile. The jokes he'd tell that weren't always funny, but because he was telling them we all laughed. Now we never talk about him. It's like he just disappeared one day and we both agreed to never mention him again. Not that we discussed it. It just played out like that.

When Dad was still around, I'd sneak into their room sometimes in the night and wiggle my way in between my sleeping parents. Mum smelt like soap and shampoo then. She always showered before bed, said it helped her sleep.

I've kept some of the doodles Dad used to scribble to me. He'd wedge them in my lunch box so that I'd find them when I was eating my cheese and cucumber sandwich with no crusts. His doodles would be silly. A face poking out a tongue. A cow mooing over a fence. And me. He drew me all the time. Of course, the drawings looked nothing like me. Just random little girls with straight bangs and rainboots on, although I always knew. I have a collection of them on my wall, just near my pillow. I say good night to them most nights.

Dad gave me a love of stories and Vegemite and watching the stars. Mum gave me her turned-up nose, her shortness, and her sometimes-sadness, but I refuse to inherit her depression, too. We both have brown eyes and brown hair and slightly freckled skin. She's taller than me but not by much. I bet Riley would probably be her height.

Mum's been off work for ten months now. She managed to work for eight months after Dad died, but then it all got too hard and her boss offered her some time off. That time off has just kept stretching and now she's on disability benefits from the government. It means money is pretty tight and there's not much to run the house or pay bills or buy shoes. In winter, we have to be careful with the heating and mostly go to bed with blankets and hot water bottles, because gas is too expensive. I don't mind the blankets. Or not having a phone. Though having some new shoes that fit my feet would be a relief.

"Mum," I whisper, edging around her bed. I make it to the blinds and start to lift them, flooding the room with sunlight.

"Leave it, Meg."

"You sure?"

"Yeah. It hurts my eyes," she says, rolling over so she's facing the wall. I let the blinds drop, sealing us back in.

She's like a vampire, existing only in darkness. I lean down, as close as I dare, and touch her arm.

"You okay, Mum?"

"Yeah. Just tired. My headache's gone. I'm sure I'll be better tonight. . . ."

"I'm heading out now."

"Have a good day, honey," she whispers. "Have you had breakfast?"

I decide to lie. "Yeah. Cereal." Of course, if she ever bothered opening the cupboard she would know that it's been a while since we've had cereal. It's a luxury item, and one we can rarely afford.

"Okay, Meg, love you. . . ."

And then like a ghost, she's gone, rolled away from me and snuggled into the bedclothes.

Sometimes it's hard to walk and breathe at the same time. I burst into the office using my hip to bang open the door. I clutch the Bag higher and closer to my mouth, using it to gasp for air. I notice the paper crinkles in and out as it shrinks and expands.

"Come through, Meg," says Sarah, walking down the corridor and opening the door to the nurse's office.

I follow her in. She plumps a pillow up on the chair in the corner and maneuvers me into it. When I'm sitting down, I lean forward so I can gulp more air.

"Breathe in . . . breathe out . . . ," says Sarah.

I suck too fast, like air is a lollipop at a party that a little kid will take away from me if I don't finish it quickly. She rubs my back and I force myself to stay within her reach. I spy the rim of dirt on the tips of my slippers where they poke out from under the chair, and hope nobody else feels the need to visit the nurse's office right now.

"I bought crumpets. Are you hungry?" she says quietly.

I nod. I can smell the roses of Sarah's perfume.

The phone rings in the office.

She stops rubbing my back. "I'll be back in a sec," she tells me.

The door opens and she taps it with her foot so that it shuts gently. And I'm alone.

It's early. The bell hasn't rung yet. Usually I'm not here quite so early. I take a normal breath and push all the air out of my lungs as hard as I can until the Bag is stretched to its limit. Then it softens. The paper walls relax and it starts to sag. I pull it away from my mouth, searching the edges. In the right-hand corner I see a tear—tiny and traitorous. I've popped a seam with all my air. Now I'm really going to need to find a new bag. And soon. I shouldn't have used it for breathing this morning, because I didn't need to, but today I'm too hungry to make it through Literature Circle.

I'm smoothing down the Bag, brushing my hand along it, flattening it so I can fold it up and take it home and add it to my drawer, when Sarah comes back in. She holds out a plate with two lightly toasted crumpets covered in honey and butter. I haven't had these for a while.

"Not too cooked, right?"

I nod, pleased she remembered I don't like the edges too

crunchy, and bite into the warm dough, dripping honey down my front onto Gumby. Luckily it's washing night tomorrow.

"How's everything going?"

"Good." I keep eating, wishing I could go slow but knowing I'll be done in seconds.

"I hear you've been picked to write one of the graduation speeches."

I look up into her concerned eyes.

"I'm sure it will be fabulous, Meg," Sarah says kindly.

Deciding to pounce on her sympathies, I hold up the now empty plate, smeared with yellow butter. "Are there any more?"

"Oh . . . still hungry?"

I can't risk her thinking I'm not eating at home, so I aim for witty. "It's because honey is my life," I tell Sarah. She looks at me oddly. Her eyes crease around the edges, like she's trying to work me out.

"Meg?"

"It's a quote from *Winnie-the-Pooh*. It was Dad's favorite," I say, feeling momentarily guilty for playing the Dad card. But then I remember the taste of crumpets and all guilt disappears.

Her eyes widen and I see the wobbly lines of black eyeliner, drawn in a hurry as if she were running late for work.

"Of course. I'll go get more crumpets," she says. "Another two?"

"Yes, please." I smile as she walks off down the corridor.

I'm pretty sure that Dad never read *Winnie-the-Pooh*. He wasn't a big reader, but he did tell me stories. Made-up ones, from his head. They were silly and funny and I remember the feeling of curling up against his warm arm to listen.

I take out *Anne of Green Gables* from my otherwise empty schoolbag and open the cover, holding it carefully so the spine doesn't crack any further. Taking a breath, I start to read; I've scanned the words so many times, I know where they all sit on the page.

The bell rings and I hear kids screaming and yelling out, stampeding their way to class. I wonder how long I can sit in here before Sarah sends me back.

The door bursts open. I look up, expecting to see my crumpets. Instead, I see blood and a girl squawking with her head back and Riley helping that girl.

Sarah rushes in behind them, and I don't know where to look. I pretend I'm still reading, though that seems callous given all the blood, so then I face the squawking and Sarah trying to find an ice pack in the fridge.

Riley has her hands in the blood, helping her friend. I can't see the face of the other girl, just the stains of red dripping down her chin and top, like her skin has split a seam.

"Here!" Sarah wraps an ice pack with paper towels and moves in front of the mess so I can't see anything.

"Press it down over the bridge," says Sarah.

"Ow! Watch it."

Three dramatic words and I know immediately that the bloodied nose belongs to Lina. I sink into the chair, trying to shrink myself so my book covers me. I can't escape. They block the only exit; I'm stuck.

Sarah steps to one side, revealing me, and of course Riley glances across at exactly the same moment. She's about to say something but stops herself, looking back to her patient and then to me. Her mouth moves slightly like there's a smile brewing, but then she turns to Lina.

"I think it's stopped bleeding," says Sarah.

"I'm going to kill Lachy! This top was an early birthday present!" Lina says, glaring at the splatter of blood ruining the crisp pale-green shirt. "Maybe I can make him buy me a new one."

"He didn't mean it," Riley says quietly.

"He needs to watch where he's kicking the stupid ball!" snaps Lina.

A phone starts ringing and I know that means Sarah is about to dash off and leave me here—with them. I move *Anne of Green Gables* up even higher.

"Back in a sec, girls," Sarah says as she disappears down the corridor.

Time seems to move too fast, like bathwater speeding in circles down the drain. With my head behind the cover of the book I can't tell if Lina has seen me. I stay as still as a statue.

"I recognize those slippers. Looks like someone is hiding from us, Riley," says Lina.

I drop the book. Lina's eyes blink with shutter speed, like she's taking a photograph of me in all my nurse's office glory.

Then a smirk slides along one side of her face, never reaching the other, and she sniffs up the blood that must have started thickening in her nostrils.

I decide to get in first. "The new look suits you, Lina," I tell her, clutching a hand across my heart to still the wild shaking in my chest.

"Oh, look, Riley, I was right. It *is* Slipper Girl. How you doing, SG?"

I've been wearing slippers for over a week now, though until Riley commented on them by the lockers last week, the rest of grade six hadn't seemed to notice. She must have told Lina about the nickname. I knew it was only a matter of time.

Riley's broken the allegiance rule of the nurse's office, and it makes my shoulders tense up, so I focus on Lina. "I'm faring somewhat better than you, I'd say."

Riley is flicking her gaze between Lina and me so fast, it's like she's watching a game of tennis.

Lina moves closer. She's taller than me, and because I'm sitting down, she's even more imposing than normal. I could stand up, but I don't want her to think I'm scared. Lina thrives on fear. She's like a tiger patrolling the schoolyard, sniffing out prey.

My mouth is coated in sticky honey and my stomach is squirming. Shame I can't vomit on command.

"Your slippers are so fetching, aren't they, R?"

R? Do they all go by single letters now? And why wasn't it cool to have one-syllable names back in grade four? I look pointedly at Riley, hoping she's not as much like Lina as Dash seems to think. But she quickly looks away and then clears her throat.

Lina grabs Riley's hand, pulling her forward until they are both towering over me.

"Don't you just wish you could wear slippers to school too, R?"

Riley fidgets with her bangs, fixing them just so. Usually Riley's hair is messier, but today she and Lina look like a neat ponytail pair. Dash is right about one thing—they have matching hairstyles.

"Yeah," she finally agrees, and I push back harder into the chair, wishing it would open up, suck me in, and deliver me to another dimension.

Lina steps even closer. "You really love hanging out in here, don't you, SG?"

I decide if she comes within reach of my leg, I'll kick her— right in the shin. I can see Riley trying to catch my eye but I refuse to give her anything. She sided with her friend. She's not worth meaningful eye contact. The Linas of this world are one thing. They are transparently mean. But the Rileys are something else. They make you hope first.

Before Lina can wind up for another attack, Sarah comes sweeping back in without my crumpets.

"Lina, I rescued a top from Lost and Found that you can wear," she says, holding up a baggy striped T-shirt.

Lina laughs. "No thanks. Maybe give it to Meg. She could do

with some clothes. Looks like she spilled her breakfast on the top she's wearing," she says sweetly.

I make the mistake of looking down and hear Lina laugh. The honey that dripped from the crumpet has spread into a shiny blob on my chest. I should have just ignored her.

"I'll clean myself up in the bathroom. It's less crowded in there!" Lina grabs Riley by the arm and pulls her from the room. The door sighs but doesn't shut. I can hear Lina's cold laugh echoing down the corridor.

I open my book, but Lina has disrupted my day so completely that even Anne with an *e* cannot soothe me.

Chapter 8

RILEY

IT'S TUESDAY AFTERNOON AND I'M shuffling around bills and school notices on the fridge, so there's room for Lina's invite. The party's in less than two weeks and I've put off asking Mum long enough. I know my chances of going are small. But I have to try, because I hate the idea of missing out again. And I can't imagine Lina will forgive me if I don't go. I'm not sure what would happen to me without Lina, Elle, and Tessa. I'd probably be as lonely as Meg, and spend my lunchtimes hanging out in the nurse's office eating Mum's carbohydrate-controlled meals. I shouldn't have let Lina make fun of Meg, but if I'd defended her then, that meanness would have found its way to me.

"You ready for your line change, Riley?" says Mum.

I stand looking at the fridge door, waiting for her to see the invite.

"It's at a hotel," she says, reading over my shoulder.

"Yeah. It looks amazing. There's a pool on the roof!"

"Sorry, honey."

She shakes her head like it's a given, and gets distracted restacking the dishwasher because apparently, nobody else in the house does it correctly.

One, two, three...

"Mum, I have to go! She's turning twelve. It's a big deal."

"Sorry, Riley," she says with a sigh. "I just don't trust you being away for a night."

"But *I'm* responsible," I tell her, trying to keep the whine out of my voice.

"Let's do your line change, then." She turns on the dishwasher and the sound of rushing water fills the kitchen. Then she walks past, expecting me to follow.

I snatch the invite off the fridge and screw it tight, hurling it into the compost bucket. It bounces out again and I have to pick it up from the bench and drop it in.

When I walk into the lounge, the Brain is sitting at the table with her laptop open, her sunglasses still on her head and her reading glasses on her face. It's not often I see my mum looking less than perfect.

"Line change?" I snap.

"You took so long, I started on my e-mails," she says.

"I'm here now," I say, more rudely than usual.

"Your sister's late," she says without looking up.

"Um, choir practice," I say.

Jenna texted me to tell Mum she'd be late, like I'm her social secretary or, worse, her excuse-maker so she doesn't have to deal directly with Mum. I know the real reason why she's late. His name's Ash and apparently he's cute with long shaggy hair and he texts her all the time. She thinks I'm clueless about it, but when you share a room, there's not much you don't know about each other.

"I just had an e-mail about diabetes camp," Mum says, turning to look at me. I can tell she's using her professional therapy face because she knows how I feel about this subject.

"I'm not going," I tell her.

"Your dad and I think it would be a great opportunity for you," she says, standing up and reaching out to rub my shoulders. Whenever Mum is trying to win an argument, she groups her and Dad together. I bet he knows nothing about it.

"Nope," I say, and step back.

"Honey, you want more freedom. This is the perfect chance for that."

"I want to go to a sleepover party, not go to camp with a bunch of kids I don't know."

"We'll talk about it later," she says, and I know there's no point arguing because if Mum makes a decision, I will never win.

I've never been to a diabetes camp before—only a diabetes field trip, and that was bad enough. One day on a bus with a bunch of super smiley, hyped-up carers who paired us off depending on what we were wearing. I had to sit next to some girl called Charlie who had piercings in her tongue and was about six years older than me. I tried to ask questions but she just grunted at me and it was one of the worst days of my life.

Even though my parents never admit it, they totally wish I was just like all the other kids. But I'm not. I have type one diabetes. I have to say "type one" because otherwise people assume I'm type two and then some of them blame you and think it's your fault because you eat too much junk food. As if. People can be so judgmental.

I've been diabetic for years now. When I first had symptoms, Mum didn't know what was wrong with me. By the time she took me to the doctor, I was hours away from diabetic ketoacidosis (or DKA, as the doctors like to call it) and I could have died. I think it still freaks her out to think about it. The thing is, even though Mum wants me to be like everyone else, she won't let me be. If it was up to her I'd be bubble-wrapped forever and stored away from potential dangers, dragged out on display when family came to visit.

I lift up my T-shirt before Mum can do it for me, and start squeezing my stomach to find a good spot for the new line to go in. Sometimes it feels like my body is a giant pincushion being stabbed by tiny metal pins. Line changes happen every few days. It's not as bad as it sounds. There's an infusion set that delivers insulin from the pump to my body, and it has a cannula that goes just below the skin on my stomach. The cannula is inserted using a needle but the needle comes out and the cannula stays in.

"Can I do it?"

Mum gives me her *Don't be ridiculous* look and grabs the line inserter, a reservoir, and insulin.

"I'd like to do it," I say quietly. I've been begging Mum to teach me how to do it myself for the past six months, but she keeps finding excuses. Who am I kidding? She'll always find excuses.

"Diabetes isn't something to take lightly. . . ."

I sigh without even knowing I'm sighing. I've heard this speech so many times that I could recite it backward underwater. "Yep. I think I know that."

"Hold your top a bit higher," she says impatiently.

Mum holds the inserter in place and presses the button, injecting the needle into my skin without me having to see it. It doesn't hurt. Tonight it just makes me sad.

I hear Jenna's key scratching in the lock like it always does, because Dad had it cut at the cheap locksmith instead of the fancy one. When she comes in she's beaming and her cheeks look pink and strong. Surely Mum can take one look at her and realize she's been doing something more exciting than choir practice.

Jenna and I look nothing alike. She's short with muscles and long dark hair, and I'm tall and thin and blond. She's like Mum and I'm like Dad.

Mum finishes up and I quickly smooth down the front of my T-shirt, not wanting my sister to see the pockets of fat that have developed near my belly button because of the insulin going in. The nurse at the hospital tried to reassure me it was a totally *normal* part of being a diabetic, but the rest of me is all skinny and stretched out, and no one else I know has that kind of puckering across their stomach.

"You're late, Jenna," says Mum, standing up.

My sister rearranges her expression and fiddles with her backpack to stall for time. I shoot her a look over Mum's shoulder, one I hope explains that I've covered for her and that she owes me for a change.

"Yeah, choir practice," she says finally. "And now I have math homework." She starts up the stairs.

"Math homework" is probably a code for going to spend the next hour texting her friends, but Mum says nothing as Jenna vanishes. If only I could waft through the house without interrogation.

"I've got homework too," I tell Mum. I dash back into the kitchen and grab the invite from the compost. Tomato seeds are stuck to it and it's a bit soggy, but I smooth it out and take it upstairs. Lina would be horrified to know that her much-loved invite spent a few minutes hanging with the potato skins and the moldy avocado.

Our bedroom is huge. It's probably one of the biggest rooms of the house, which is how we came to still be sharing. A long brown leather couch my parents bought when they first got married divides the room. Jenna has the left side and I have the right. Sometimes at night when I can't sleep, the sound of my sister breathing or snoring makes me feel safe. She keeps threatening to move downstairs into the study, and every time she says it my heart speeds up like when I'm having a high. I'd hate it if she wasn't here, but of course I can't tell her that. I have to be all casual about it, like I don't care what room she sleeps in.

Jenna's already kicked off her shoes and pulled on an old pair of pajama pants and she's curled up on her bed with her laptop open and headphones on. I edge around the couch and step on enemy territory. She looks up at me and slowly shakes her head, warning me not to come much closer.

I reach forward and snatch the headphones from her ears, tangling the cord in her hair and causing her to yelp as she tries to pull the strands free.

"What the— Riley?"

"Sorry," I tell her, dropping the headphones and sitting down on the edge of her bed.

She finishes untangling her hair as her phone beeps. I watch her eyes read the screen, and a smile washes across her face.

"Jenna?"

"Yeah?" She's now texting back, not looking at me.

There are so many things I want to ask her, but none seem like they're solid candidates for questions she'd happily answer.

"Choir practice?"

She laughs and tosses her phone back down. I wait for her to confide in me, to tell me the real reason she was home late. Instead, she picks at the edge of her fingernails and I see the skin's all scabbed and red. She's been doing that since she was little. It drives Mum wild.

I touch her finger to stop the scratching and she gazes up slowly, like a sleepy lizard.

"Mum won't let me go to Lina's sleepover," I say, knowing she's the only person I can tell this to.

"Mum won't let you do anything."

"True."

"We have to get that figured out before junior high," she says. Her phone beeps again and I wait for her to lose interest in me. But she tucks her legs up underneath her and watches me.

"What do you want?"

It's not a question I get asked very often. "I want freedom."

Jenna doesn't laugh, which makes me love her more than usual.

"Okay. We have to begin Operation Lying Riley," she says with a smile.

I smile back and clock that she's wearing more than one stud in her left ear. "Did you get another piercing?"

She touches her ear and then nods. "Yeah. Left ear only."

"Does Mum know?"

"Does Mum care?"

"You're so lucky," I say, flopping down on her bed.

"We need to find you a hobby that she thinks is important so you can pretend that's where you are," says Jenna.

"I have netball but she always comes to the games! And she's never going to let me do any of the things I want to do. Like roller derby or soccer. She'd worry too much about my pump being knocked."

Jenna shrugs. "Maybe something that's not a contact sport?"

"Like choir?"

"Yes. Exactly."

"I can't sing," I say.

She shrugs and then I remember that she can't, either. In fact, her voice is even more out of tune than mine.

"Are you actually in a choir?"

"Sometimes."

I laugh. "Okay, so what will Mum let me do?"

"That's the problem," says Jenna dramatically.

"She wants me to go to diabetes camp."

"Shudder," says Jenna.

"Yep."

"But it might be fun. . . ."

I stare at my sister, trying to make the second piercing in her ear suddenly explode. I thought she was on my side. "No. It won't be fun. It'll suck."

Jenna shrugs and I know my time is coming to an end. Her phone has started beeping again. She picks it up and starts texting and I accept that my window has closed. I go to thank her for her advice but she's pulled her headphones back on and can't even hear me.

"Riley, set the table, please," shouts Mum from the bottom of the stairs.

"What about Jenna? It's her turn," I yell.

"I asked you!" Mum lobs back.

Obviously, Jenna hears me complaining about her because

she gives me a sarcastic one-sided grin as I leave the room.

"Hey, Riley," Dad says when I stomp into the dining room. He's sitting at one end of the table, checking his e-mail on his laptop. He's only just come home. How can he have more e-mails?

"Hey, Dad."

"Good day?" He shuts his laptop and looks up.

I shrug. "Okay."

Dad doesn't baby me like Mum does. He sort of goes along with Mum but he doesn't often get involved. Besides, if he got worried about every hospital appointment I had, he'd be even balder than he already is. With him I do things, like play card games, kick a soccer ball, go for a walk. He's the reason I can play guitar. And also the reason my guitar stays tuned.

"Quick game of UNO?"

Dad loves UNO. Me? I can take it or leave it. But he always seems disappointed if I say no.

"No time," Mum calls from the kitchen. "Dinner in a minute."

Dad winks at me, amused that Mum is listening in on our conversation from the next room.

I toss the cutlery wildly onto the table, resenting the fact that Jenna once again gets away with doing nothing.

"Taking it out on the forks, Riley?" Dad asks, straightening up my effort, and almost earning a smile.

"Actually, I want to talk to you," I tell him. "About Lina's sleepover party."

"I already said no," calls Mum from the kitchen.

"I have two parents!" I call back.

Dad smiles at me, and inside I'm quietly high-fiving him. "What's the party?"

As fast as I can, before Mum can storm in and shut me down, I tell him. About the fancy hotel, the breakfast, the in-house movies.

"Sounds impressive," says Dad, cleaning one of the forks on his work shirt.

"Her mother doesn't understand diabetes," says Mum, barging into the dining room with a large pan of steaming fish curry.

"Lina is Riley's best friend," says Dad, stabbing a piece of fish from the pan and eating it. "Maybe we don't need to criticize her mother, Tina."

I wait for Mum to snap at him. She hates it when he starts sampling the food before dinner's been served. Actually, she seems to hate lots of things that he does.

"Get the rice, Marcus," Mum says in her frustrated-doctor voice that she loves using.

I pull at my plastic diabetes alert band that always confuses the netball umpires. Each week they tell me to take it off, and each week Mum storms across to explain that I can't. If I collapse then the EMTs need to know what's wrong with me. She's been telling them this all season and you'd think they could just remember. It is pretty humiliating that Mum has to save me from them every week.

"You can invite Lina here for a night and we can take her out somewhere for her birthday," says Mum, turning her attention to me as she starts dishing up plates of food.

"No. It's not the same, Mum. I have to be there," I say, hating how whiny and high-pitched my voice sounds.

"You're not staying overnight at a hotel without one of us," says Mum, finishing spooning the curry into four bowls.

As Dad comes back, I risk a look at him, hoping he understands my silent plea for help. I can't tell Lina that my parents won't let me come. It's a social disaster. And I've pulled the sick card so many times lately that I'm amazed my friends still invite me anywhere.

"What about if I pick her up early?" asks Dad.

"What's the point in going, then?" Mum says.

"Yeah, Dad can pick me up early. At eleven," I say quickly.

"There's no point in going if you aren't sleeping over," she says.

"Please, Mum," I beg, imagining all the hours that I'll miss out on.

"Nine," says Dad. "She can have dinner and watch a movie and then I'll bring her home."

Mum looks at me, and I can see her considering the idea. Nine isn't great but it's better than nothing.

I hold my breath, thinking she might actually agree to it.

Finally she nods, and I grin at Dad, mouthing my thanks to him.

"No swimming," she tells me. "I don't want you disconnecting your pump."

"Okay."

"And I need to know what you're eating so I can work out all the grams," she says.

"I can work out the grams," I tell her, imagining how Lina's mum is going to feel about writing out a menu plan.

"No, Riley. If you want to go, you work with me on this. Okay?"

I nod. I'll agree to anything if she lets me go. Six hours are better than nothing, and I know I have to take my small victories where I can.

"And you're going to diabetes camp," she says quietly.

Something snaps in my head. "No. I'm not!" I yell.

"Riley!" Mum snaps back.

"Sorry. I didn't mean to yell."

"Why don't you want to go?" Dad asks, sampling the curry again.

I try to work out what to say, how to frame it so he understands. Then I give up and plough in.

"Just because I'm diabetic doesn't mean I want to hang out with other diabetics. Having diabetes in common isn't going to make us friends," I tell him.

"But you might enjoy being the same as everyone else," says Mum.

Sometimes I fear for her patients. It's like she sees the world as a series of Venn diagrams where we are only connected to the people we share traits with. In Mum's head I'm not like everyone else. I'm in the curve for the diabetics, and a smaller curve for the diabetics with blonde hair who happen to be good at public speaking and play a mean game of netball.

I decide to speak to Dad and sort of ignore Mum. "Diabetes isn't something we share. It's not who I am. It's just a tiny part of me," I say, feeling like I can finally explain myself properly. "Dad, you don't go to a camp for men who work in accounting," I tell him.

"But I wish I could. All those number games and trust exercises with tax exemptions!" He laughs. "That would be hideous!" he says more seriously.

"Yep . . . ," I say.

Jenna whacks me on the back of the head as she walks in. She stands near my chair and raises an eyebrow.

"That's my chair, kid," she says like I'm ten years younger, not two.

"Not tonight, *kid*," I say.

Mum takes the spoon from me before I can scoop some more brown rice into my bowl. "Leave room for salad, Riley. Jenna, sit down."

"I'm waiting for Riley to move."

"Jenna," Mum barks.

"Fine."

Jenna slams past me and sits down next to Dad. I smile as discreetly as I can and she gives me the finger. Just the usual dinnertime routine.

"Put in forty-five grams for dinner," Mum says, looking across at my plate.

I put in forty. I know my body. I know my diabetes. Tonight, I'm doing it my way.

Chapter 9

MEG

TUNA'S ON SALE SO I grab ten tins. I don't really like tuna much, because it reminds me of the cat we used to have, but it makes for an easy dinner, so I eat it.

We also need baked beans and muesli bars and a bag of carrots and some apples. I grab a brown paper mushroom bag, too, because I need a new one for my breathing. It's not as strong as I'd like, but it'll do until I can find a better one.

Mum doesn't go food shopping anymore, so she gives me a shopping list and her ATM card so I can access her disability payment that goes into her account on Wednesday mornings. Mum says it's good for my math skills if I shop like this. I have to add things as I go to make sure I have enough money at the end. I can only use fifty dollars and it doesn't go very far, but I usually make it work.

I was hoping the supermarket would stock shoes, but they

only have flip-flops, and I'm not sure that they'd be any better than wearing slippers to school. Now that Lina's started calling me Slipper Girl, I'm probably stuck with it. And it's not like I have enough money to buy shoes anyway.

I toss a couple of packets of Cup-a-Soup and a loaf of white bread into the basket. It takes a minute to add it all up in my head. The numbers swarm and then fix when I can imagine them standing columns like my brain is a fancy calculator. There's enough money left over for a packet of the cream biscuits Mum likes, and a small bag of candy for me.

I generally keep my head down in the supermarket after school. There are so many faces I spend my day avoiding, and it's worse if I see them here. I hate them checking out what's in my basket and seeing what I buy. But for some reason, as I stand in front of the candy display, I choose that moment to look up and down the aisle. Maybe it's instinct, because I'm not a big believer in fate, but right at that second, Riley Jackson looks down the aisle and spies me as I spy her.

It's a Western-style standoff, both of us ready to shoot first. Although instead of shooting, I turn and flee, hurrying away from her, back down the aisle toward the checkout.

"Meg!"

I speed up, passing the candy so fast it's just a blur of color and sugar. After what's been happening at school, where her friends all laugh whenever I walk past and Lina makes jokes about my slippers, I have nothing to say to her.

I've nearly made it to the end of the aisle when she careers around me and swings her cart across, blocking me in. For a second I'm not sure she's going to stop. Maybe she'll slam the cart into me and its wheels will flatten my body into the shiny white floor, and she and Lina will celebrate by eating all of the crumpets and honey that Sarah usually feeds me.

"Hey," she says.

I start to push past her, trying to get around the side. I'm weighing up how polite I have to be. It's not like she's given me any reason to be, but direct rudeness is not something I encourage. "I'm in a hurry," I tell her.

"Just wanted to say hi," she says, sounding almost genuine.

I look up, noticing her blue eyes and messy ponytail. I'm not as intimidated by her here as I am at school when she has her friends around her, but I still don't want to stand around making small talk.

"Excuse me," says a man behind me.

"Sorry." Riley moves her cart to the side, and lets him squeeze past.

"Are you apologizing to me?" I say.

"What?" she says.

"Slipper Girl?" I can just imagine Dash shaking his head at me. And he'd be right. Why am I engaging with this? Don't I know better? Didn't I learn anything from Eleanora?

"We were just mucking around, Meg. My friends . . ."

"Aren't very nice?"

"They are sometimes," she says defensively.

I pull a face, hoping it conveys just how suspicious I am of

88

that being true. "I can think of plenty of words to describe Lina. 'Nice' isn't one of them."

I'm surprised when she laughs and I find myself liking the sound. I have to keep remembering what Dash said. She is one to avoid.

"You're probably right. But she is my friend."

"Good luck with that," I say, starting to edge away. Then I stop. "And you're part of it, Riley. I didn't hear you telling Lina to stop."

She nods and looks at the ground. "Yeah . . . sorry."

"It's all very well to read about sorrows, but not so nice when you have to live through them," I tell her, knowing I haven't remembered the quote correctly, but knowing it doesn't matter anyway. She's obviously not a kindred spirit.

"What?"

"You wouldn't understand." I keep pushing past her.

But instead of letting me go, she peers into my basket. "Wow, you must really like tuna," she says lightly.

I snatch away my basket so she can't see the rest of my shopping.

Riley touches my arm. "Just making small talk, Meg."

"I don't do small talk," I tell her. "I have to go."

"Is your mum here too?" Riley looks around as if she expects to see a mum trailing behind.

I shake my head, concentrating on the display of chocolate biscuits on sale.

"So, you get to do the shopping?"

I nod, and sneak a look across at her. Her blue eyes widen and she sighs like she's imagining a trip to Disneyland or something.

"You're so lucky," she tells me.

"Oh, yes. Lucky, that's me."

"My mum checks every single packet before she even considers buying it. She has this app on her phone that tells her carbohydrates for everything. It's all about health. When I come shopping with her, it can take hours," she says dramatically.

Then she reaches across and grabs a packet of jelly beans from the end of the display and drops it into my basket.

"I can pick my own candy, thank you very much," I say, putting them back, and choosing something different, even though her choice was probably one I would have made if they didn't cost so much.

She fidgets and looks around. "Do you walk to school?"

"What's with all the questions?" I snap.

She pulls a face. "Sorry. Just trying to be friendly."

"Yes, I walk to school. I live down the road with my mum. She likes tuna; I don't," I say in the flattest voice I can manage. "Is that enough?"

She rocks the cart back and forth, unaware that a woman is trying to get past.

"You might want to move," I tell her.

She grins at the woman as she walks by and I see how easily Riley navigates situations. Even me. I need to get out of here.

"I'm not allowed to walk anywhere on my own," she continues. "It's only, like, a ten-minute walk to school. Mum drives me everywhere!"

"We don't have a car. I have to walk," I say.

"Cool. Environmentalists," she says.

I bite down a smile, thinking how surprised Riley would be if I deflated her assumptions.

"Do you have a phone?"

"No," I tell her.

"So, you walk yourself to school and do the shopping and your mum can't even call you?" she says.

I nod.

She sighs and leans against the cart. "That's what it's like for Lina, too. She has so much freedom. I can't do anything!"

Nobody has ever envied me. How does Riley not know that? I wonder what she'd say if she knew my life is miserable at best and the only reason I walk everywhere alone is because my mum never leaves the house.

"There you are, Riley. I thought I said aisle nine," says a voice behind me.

"Sorry, Mum! I've just been talking to Meg."

Riley's mum steps around so that she's in front of me. I wait for her to look me up and down, to notice my slippers, and to not care that I notice her noticing. But she doesn't. She keeps her eyes on my face. She has the same sparkling blue eyes that her daughter has, though that's where the similarities end.

She's wearing a suit and heels and her dark hair is up and slick and smooth. She looks corporate and in control.

"Hi, Meg. I'm Tina," she says, holding her hand out so I can shake it.

I swallow hard and slide my hand into my pocket. I just need to feel the corner of the mushroom bag first. Then I pull my hand out and shake hers as quickly as possible and let go, returning my hand to the pocket with the mushroom bag where it feels safe.

"Meg's mum lets her do the shopping. And she gets to walk to school on her own! I was just telling her how lucky she is!"

"It's not a big deal. Mum's just busy. . . ."

"Are you two at school together?" asks Riley's mum.

"Yeah . . . Meg's in grade six, too," says Riley. "We're both doing graduation speeches," she adds.

My other hand is getting clammy, so I clutch the handle of the plastic basket as tight as I can.

"That's quite an honor, Meg," says Riley's mum.

Riley laughs. "She doesn't think so. Meg thinks it's just a chance to 'brag about yourself,'" she says, making little quotation marks with her fingers.

I'm so surprised that Riley remembered what I said to Ms. Barber that I forget to respond. Riley's mum joins in the laugh. "I tend to agree with you, Meg. Graduating from elementary school does seem a little . . . unnecessary."

"I'd better go," I say. "It was nice to meet you."

"We can drop you home," says Riley, stepping closer to me.

"No thank you," I say. "I like walking."

I catch a glimpse of Riley's mum watching me, reading me.

"We have more shopping to do, Riley. Nice to meet you, Meg," she says to me.

I nod at her, relieved that she saved me so easily. I scurry around the corner of the aisle, then stop and peek back at them, making sure they don't see me. I notice the way Riley's mum takes the cart from Riley and together they wheel away down the aisle. They don't look alike but they look together, like they belong, walking in step through the supermarket. They slow and Riley's mum bends down slightly so she can hear whatever her daughter is saying. I wait until they turn the corner at the end of the aisle before I head for the checkout.

I start throwing all my shopping onto the belt before anyone else can beat me. I touch the corner of the Bag in my pocket just for reassurance. Then I unzip my backpack and toss the things in as the young guy scans them.

"Forty-nine fifty," he says in a nasally voice.

He takes my crisp fifty-dollar note that doesn't have any creases and holds it up to the light, like maybe I'm some sort of counterfeit expert.

I take my change and lift my backpack. It's never heavy, except on shopping days, and today it weighs me down more than usual. I head for the glass doors, relieved that I'm escaping the supermarket and fleeing the scene. As I go I realize that

I still don't know why Riley went to the nurse's office, and I just lost my chance to ask her.

I'm still thinking about Riley and her mum as I set the table in the dining room. About how light they were together, how they involved each other in the conversation. There's something about Riley that's different to the other girls. I can't imagine Lina or Tessa trying to talk to me in the supermarket.

I fill the water glasses and place mine down over the scratching in the wood. This was Dad's childhood table and he carved his initials into it when he was a kid. I always sit where the carving is. JKT: JIM KIERAN TOWER.

Heading to the window, I tug on the cord to open the blinds. I can't risk drawing them back completely because Mum doesn't like it, though a scrap of sunshine should be okay. Then I force the rusted lock, the metal digging into my fingers, and slide the window open just enough so there's a breeze.

The back garden is overgrown with weeds and grass that skirts my knees. Every few months or so, Dave at number thirty-two pops over and mows for us without bothering to ask Mum. I let him in down the side and he tidies up a bit, too. It's not the haven it was when Dad was here, when Mum and Dad both spent hours gardening on the weekends, but it's strangely beautiful out there. The trees are overgrown and need a trim, but they make me feel cocooned, like I'm surrounded and nobody can see in.

We never ate inside during summer with Dad, because he

loved dining outdoors. He'd light the barbecue and cook a tray of chops and sausages, disappearing behind a veil of smoke. Dinner with Dad was never just a meal. It was always a feast.

Now the backyard is my space. Mum doesn't often go out there. I think it reminds her too much of Dad and she avoids those memories. I try to find them wherever I can: in a postcard still stuck to the fridge from when he went to visit his brother one year; in the gnarled and ancient lemon tree that Dad used to prune; and even in the old record player that used to spin crackling songs on the weekends and now remains closed.

This room is so dusty. Our house didn't always look like this. Once it was full of flowers picked from the garden and the windows were open and the blinds up. There was always air and light and laughter in the rooms. When Dad was alive, Eleanora used to come for playdates and we'd lie on the floor in my room giggling and sharing secrets, and Mum would cook us a stack of pancakes and we'd eat them with our fingers.

Mum shuffles into the room carrying our plates and places one in front of me. Once it would have been a real meal, but now it's just a tin of tuna, spinach from the garden, two slices of bread, and some pieces of apple. I bet Riley's mum cooks. Elaborate meals with vegetables and they all sit around talking about their days. I bet she never eats fish from a tin.

"Dinner is served!" Mum's voice is light, but her eyes give her away.

"Yum, thanks," I say, playing along. At least Mum has plated food up tonight. The last few weeks it's been left to me.

She sits down opposite me. She's still in her old paint-stained T-shirt from when she cared about the house, and the stretched black tracksuit pants she wears most days. I make her change out of them on Tuesdays so I can wash her things with mine when I visit Peggy. I bet Riley's mum never wears the same clothes for a week.

"How was school today?"

"Fine," I say quietly. "I aced the math test."

She smiles at me. "You always do."

She's wrong. I don't. Not always. Once or twice I've struggled with decimals, although Mum isn't big on details. I pull back the ring on the tin of tuna.

Our neighbors have music playing and I can hear someone singing along. They don't talk to us much now. They came to Dad's funeral and made casseroles for a while, and left them on the front step. But then Mum didn't recover, and I think they gave up.

"Mum, can you sign my school forms? I have to take them in." I've been hoping that she'd do it without me asking. I left the envelope near her bed, but she didn't even open it.

"Can't believe you'll be at junior high next year," she says, reaching for my hand across the table.

Her skin is warm and soft and for a second, her touch drags me under, as I remember how she used to hold my hand sometimes when we walked to school.

"It doesn't seem that long ago . . . ," she whispers. She looks up at me and I see the face that is so like mine. The brown eyes that appear sad even when she says she's not. She's skinny, all edges and lines. Her elbows jut out and her collarbone is so sharp, like someone has pegged her body on the line and left her there too long.

"Mum, I'll need a uniform for junior high," I say as I pull my hand clear. "And shoes."

She nods and takes a big breath.

"Maybe we could go shopping together?" I say, knowing it might trigger something.

She nods at me, but her gaze darts away. "Soon, Meg."

Soon isn't a date. It's not even a month. It's just a future that I can't pin down. I concentrate on the tuna, the oil glistening on the plate. Riley probably has her junior high uniform already pressed and hanging in her wardrobe, ready for the big day.

I hear Mum's breath quicken. She leaps up, her leg bumping the table. Water spills from our glasses. "I forgot the salt. Back in a sec."

I watch her scurry away, and then scrape the last fragments of tuna into my mouth.

There's a crash in the kitchen and the light pops and dies, leaving me at the mercy of the last rays of sunlight coming in through the window. Mum's shorted the electricity again. I never used to like the dark. It used to scare me. Although now I'm in it so often that I don't mind. The electrician came a few months ago, but he said it was a wiring issue and it would cost thousands to fix properly. Unsurprisingly, we now just change fuses and cross our fingers.

I bite into the apple, the taste not as sweet as I'd hoped, and head off to check on Mum. From the hallway I hear her breathing, raspy and forced, the sound ugly and private. I peep around the edge of the doorframe, and see her crouched against the cupboards, her body huddled and small, her mouth over a paper bag. The bag shrinks and stretches with each breath.

I wonder what Riley would do if she found her mum hiding out in the kitchen trying to breathe. Would she rush in and rub her back, calming her until her muscles softened and the air came back? Or would she just stand and watch?

Actually, I know the answer. Riley wouldn't have to do anything because her mum is in the world. She's not shorting fuses and forgetting to fill in forms, and wearing the same clothes every day. She's working and shopping and laughing about graduation with her daughter, and even if sometimes in a quiet moment she feels as bleak as my mum does, she deals with it herself. And Riley can get on with her life.

Chapter 10

RILEY

I DON'T USUALLY HAVE NURSE appointments on Thursdays, but now, thanks to the Hulk, here I am. Dad doesn't normally do hospital visits. That's Mum's area, but she had to see a patient this morning. Dad's in his suit because this isn't supposed to take long. We traipse past families crowding around a tank of brightly colored fish.

"Hot chocolate before we go in, Riley?"

"Only if it comes with marshmallows," I tell him, imagining Mum's reaction if she knew Dad was offering me hot chocolate.

He leaves me near the lifts and heads to Mum's favorite café. I'm surrounded by the noise of other people's families. Little kids run past, being chased by parents with babies in strollers. Everyone here is like me. Different. Maybe Mum's right. Maybe there is no such thing as normal. Then I see a kid being pushed in a wheelchair. He has no hair. I wonder if he's got cancer or some other illness that needs chemo. He sees me watching and sticks out his tongue and I feel like I'm a tourist checking out the fish in the tank. I want to apologize as he passes. Tell him I know how he feels. But I don't. I'm well. I'm healthy.

I do a blood glucose test quickly before Dad comes back. I'm sure people are looking at me, hunched over and squeezing blood onto the test strip, but I don't mind them staring in here.

"One pink, one white," says Dad, holding out a plastic take-away cup with two crusty marshmallows perched on top.

"Thanks," I tell him, unzipping my fanny pack and taking out my pump.

"Dad, grams?"

He frowns like he's trying to remember numbers in his head. Finally he answers and I halve it and punch the number in, knowing I won't drink all of this before my appointment. I slurp the top of the cup and feel the too-hot milk scald my throat. A girl about my age hobbles past on crutches. She's on her own and wearing a slipper on one foot and nothing on the other. If she weren't so tall, she'd sort of remind me of Meg.

Dad's quiet as he drinks his latte with two sugars. I spy a brown paper bag and know that means he's bought something sweet, too.

"Dad?"

"Yeah?"

"I'm the only one at my school who isn't allowed to go shopping without parents." I think back to meeting Meg in the supermarket.

"Do you want to?"

"What do you think?"

He looks across at me and I see the frown beginning. I know he's searching for words that he's heard Mum use.

"Don't say no. Please. I'm responsible. This is about me."

He nods. I'm not sure if that means anything but it's better than all of Mum's excuses.

"Please just think about it," I say quietly before swallowing the half-melted pink marshmallow in one lumpy gulp.

"Come on, we should go."

I toss the rest of my hot chocolate into the bin. It lands heavily on the mountain of the white takeaway cups, splashing hot chocolate in a messy spread.

This is normal. There is no normal.

"Pat's away today," says some guy with a cheesy smile. "So you get me instead!"

I groan. I hate seeing the replacements. Especially ones wearing bright blue shirts that match the friendly furniture.

"Come on, Riley," Dad says, following the nurse.

We walk into the room off the hallway and the guy shuts the door behind us. This room is worse than some of the others. For a start, it has coral-colored walls, and it's cramped with three people. It means when we all sit, our knees almost touch, reminding me of the school nurse's office.

The nurse's security tag hangs low around his neck. Pat

always puts hers on the desk, but maybe this guy wants me to know he's important.

"I'm Tony," he says, still smiling. His teeth are amazingly white.

"Hi, Tony. I'm Paul and this is Riley."

"I was just looking at Riley's levels. They're a bit up and down," he says to Dad. He's obviously missed the Pediatric Nursing 1o1 class if he thinks he should be speaking to the parent instead of the patient.

I cough loudly, reminding Tony that I'm in the room too. "Yeah, well, it can be hard at school, and apparently, the reason I'm here is because of my levels being 'a bit up and down,'" I say, imitating his words.

Now he looks up at me. He nods, but his eyes give him away. "It looks like you have binge periods, Riley. Maybe you gobble, gobble, gobble whatever's in front of you without thinking."

He tries for a laugh after this, like we will actually find this funny.

I hold my breath, hoping my dad won't join in. He doesn't. Instead, he reaches forward and places his hand on my shoulder.

"I think if Riley says it can be hard at school, then it can be hard at school," says Dad.

Tony looks up and shrugs. "Of course. I wasn't trying to upset anyone. We're just aiming for consistency and it's important she's aware of what she eats."

"She's aware of what she eats," says Dad.

Normally I'd hate Dad speaking for me. But today it's

strangely reassuring to have him on my side. Pat never does this. She never lectures me about food or sugar or how I choose to do things. She might help me look at something that's a problem and find a way through it together, but she never pulls this.

"I thought we could look at your daily diet," he says.

Now it's my turn to laugh. "What's a daily diet? I don't have one. Except soup. But the rest of the time I just eat food. Like everyone else."

"Yes, but around this age—"

"Thanks, Tony," interrupts Dad. "I think we'll come back and see Pat when she's in. Riley has a special relationship with her and it might be easier to talk through all this then."

Tony starts to say something but Dad is already on his feet.

"Let's go, Riley."

I jump up, delighted to be bailing already and wishing I could stick my tongue out at Tony.

Tony mumbles something but by then Dad has already opened the door and I've hurried out behind him.

We make it to the lift before Dad looks at me and grins goofily. "Feel like some lunch? I'd like to gobble something up. What about you?"

I laugh. "Yep. Dumplings!"

"Sounds good!"

The lift doors open and Dad and I walk forward and stand in the middle.

"Mum's going to be cross," I tell him.

He shrugs. "Probably. But that's okay."

"Really?"

"That guy was a fool. Your mum would have left too."

I lean against Dad's arm, knowing he's wrong. I can hear his phone pinging in his pocket, announcing an e-mail. I wait for him to move me and slide his hand in, but instead he drapes his arm around my shoulder.

There's a dumpling restaurant at the hospital that Mum always hurries past and never lets me go to. Dad holds my hand as we walk in and find a table.

"What are you having?"

"Pork buns and chicken dumplings," I tell Dad.

"Sounds good to me."

Dad goes to the counter to order, leaving me to think about Tony and his gobble comment. I wonder what Meg would have said if she'd been here.

I'm playing with the bottle of soy sauce as he returns with two plates stacked high. I grab a pork bun before he even sits down. Then I put it on my plate and do a test before I start eating. I see Dad notice but I'm relieved that he doesn't comment. I'm trying to show him how responsible I am.

"How many grams, do you reckon?" I say, waving my hand across the food on the table. It can be hard trying to work out how many grams are in foods you don't eat all the time. It's not like there are any carbohydrate listings on the back of a plate of dumplings.

"What do you think?" Dad asks.

I look up, surprised. I put in the number I think is right and then I peel the rice paper off from underneath and pick at the fluffy white dough.

"I love these," Dad says, biting the end of the chicken dumpling. "I could eat a hundred!"

The soupy stuff on the inside spurts out of his dumpling and runs straight down his white shirt.

"Dad . . . you dribbled!"

He looks down and sees the stain. Then he shrugs like he doesn't care.

"I've got a spare shirt at work." He looks up and it's like looking at Jenna. They have the same intense green eyes.

"Can I have the last pork bun?" I ask him.

"If I can have the last chicken dumpling," he says.

"Deal." And we shake hands to seal it.

After Dad drops me off at school, I walk to my classroom and look through the window. I see Lina, Elle, and Tessa hunched together at a table with a large sheet of A3 paper in front of them. Lina is writing with a Sharpie and the others are watching her. I wait for one of them to look up and see me standing outside, and to wave me in, but they don't. Usually I don't mind going back to school after my hospital appointments, but today, looking at my friends, I just feel so different and I don't want to go in. They're all wearing matching T-shirts with a large sequin heart on the front that changes color if you run your hand up and flip the sequins over. I begged Mum for one, but she said I had enough clothes. I look down at the T-shirt I'm wearing. It's an old one of Jenna's that says GRANGER in faded black letters from her Harry Potter phase, and for some reason it reminds me of Meg's Gumby T-shirt. And suddenly I want to see her.

I smile when I see Meg curled up on her chair in the corner. She has a small bag of chocolate biscuits on her lap and seems to be slowly working through the lot. Remembering what Meg told me about the germy bed, I look quickly across at the sheets to see if they've been washed. They look clean, but I'm also pretty sure they were white sheets last time, too.

"Hey," I say, letting the door shut behind me.

"Hi," she says, waving. The ends of her fingers are covered in chocolate.

I wait for her to look away but she doesn't; she holds my gaze like she's trying to work something out. Meg has one of those curious faces. Sort of striking because her features are all so perfect, but then also totally forgettable because she doesn't accentuate them. If Lina had Meg's features, they'd be covered in makeup and she wouldn't have messy hair that hides part of her face.

I'm careful as I sit down not to bump against Meg's legs. It's pretty cozy in here today. I notice that Meg isn't wearing the Gumby T-shirt. This new T-shirt is a bit faded and the unicorn looks like it's losing its horn, but it suits her somehow.

"How you doing?" I ask.

"Biscuit?" She holds out the bag and doesn't answer my question.

"That's funny. Most people never offer me sweet stuff. People are weird about offering me sugar. They don't really understand how it all works."

I see Meg frown and I realize she has no idea what I'm talking about. How is that possible?

Meg sits forward. "Why?"

"I'm diabetic," I tell her, leaning against the wall.

"Oh, so that's what's wrong with you," she says, nibbling off tiny pieces of biscuit.

"It's not 'what's wrong' with me!" I snap at her.

She pulls a face, surprised at my tone. "My apologies."

I don't know why, but I thought it would be different with her. I thought she'd understand. I thought that maybe I could even do tests in front of her like I could with my old friends without her making a big deal out of it. I go to leave, deciding that talking to her is just as bad as talking to Tony, the replacement nurse, or worse, my mum.

"Is that why you carry candy?" she asks quietly when I reach the door.

Sighing, I turn around. "Yeah. Did you think I just have a stash because I love sugar?"

Meg nods and her bangs bob up and down. Something about how eager she looks makes me laugh. "What about you? Why are you here?"

"I am positively famished."

It's not what I expected. I don't know what to say. I wait for her to joke about it or make light of it or something, but she keeps nibbling the biscuits like she's trying to make them last as long as possible. I scan her body trying to see if she's super skinny, but she sort of looks like me.

"Anorexia?" I whisper the word that I don't truly understand.

It's her turn to laugh so loud that biscuit crumbs snort from her nose and land in the space between us.

"No. I'm hungry. Actually hungry. And I rather like the quiet in here," she says, watching me again.

"Is that why you have that paper bag with you? The one I saw the other day. Does it have food in it?"

Meg reaches into her pocket and pulls out a mushroom bag. It's different from the plain one she had the other day. She looks at it, like she's remembering it's there. Then she shakes her head. "No."

I wait for her to explain, but she returns to the biscuits.

"It's not that quiet in here. What about the hum of the fridge?" I ask, wanting suddenly to draw her out.

She shrugs. "I don't mind that."

"Do you want me to go?"

She shrugs again, so I lean back against the chair, making the vinyl squeak.

Meg smirks. "That noise is fine too."

She holds out the biscuits again and this time I take one. Mum never lets me eat these.

"What does diabetes feel like?"

Plenty of people have asked me what it feels like to have a low or a high. They think it's the same as when they eat too much sugar at a party and feel all buzzy. It's not. It's different every time and it's not something I can explain or make sense of. Sometimes, diabetes makes me feel heavy and slow. Other times it's not like that at all.

"It's kind of impossible to explain. It's not any one thing. It changes."

Meg licks her finger and collects the tiniest of crumbs from the plate.

"Have you written your graduation speech yet?" I ask.

She reaches across and balances the plate on top of the medicine fridge. "I don't care about all that."

"What? Elementary school? Graduation? Junior high?"

"Any of it."

"How come?"

"It doesn't affect me," she says in a voice that's edged and hard.

"You planning on staying at elementary school forever?"

She smiles at me now, and I'm not sure if she finds me funny or ridiculous.

"It's not like anyone doesn't graduate from elementary school," she says.

I laugh. I'd never thought of it like that before. "Jasper Mayne might not."

"True. The way he's going, he'll be suspended."

"I wish. He's so rude."

"We were friends once," Meg says in a quiet voice that makes me want to ask her questions.

"Are you really not going to graduation?"

Meg nods, making her bangs flop forward. I hadn't noticed the spray of freckles across her nose before. They're really pale, like someone has scrubbed them clean.

"Don't your parents want you to go?"

"Dad's dead. Mum's . . . busy," she says.

"Oh. Sorry," I tell her, feeling awkward. I can't help but wonder how it feels to have no father. Even my grandparents are still alive. Nobody I know has a parent who's died. I don't know what to say, so I use Mum's breathing trick. *One, two, three . . .* I want to offer her more than an apology but nothing comes.

"I wear slippers because I've outgrown my shoes," Meg says quietly. Then she screws up the empty biscuit packet and tosses it toward the bin in the corner. It misses.

"Your turn," she says.

I want to ask her about the slipper thing, but she obviously doesn't want to discuss it any further. Now I'm not sure if it's my turn to tell her a secret or to throw the packet. I stand up and grab it.

"My mum won't let me do anything," I say, sitting down and tossing the packet at the bin. It falls short.

Meg moves fast, snatching it up and returning to her seat, like a zippy little ringtail possum.

"I like pretending that the nurse's office is my home," she says, hurling the packet toward the wall. This time it slams straight into the bin.

"Nice shot."

"Thanks."

I have other questions, but without the game I can't ask them. Instead, I watch Meg open the cupboard and dig around inside. She pulls out a pair of plastic cups. One has MEG written on it. The other says DASH.

"Drink?"

"Sure," I say, sort of expecting a stash of lemonade to come out too. I'm disappointed when she uses the nurse's office tap to fill the cups, and holds the DASH one out to me.

"Thanks."

We sip in sync. She finishes her water and instead of binning the cup, she rinses it and returns it to the cabinet.

"Who's Dash?"

"A kid in grade five . . ."

"Elle's brother?"

"That's the one."

I smile, liking the fact Meg uses old-fashioned words and sayings. She plucks the cup from my hand, washes it out, and adds it to the cupboard with hers.

"Bet nobody else cleans up in here," I say.

"I'm sure Sarah rewashes everything anyway. She hates germs," says Meg, hanging up the hand towel and tidying the basket of books. "I just make it nice. I know it's silly."

The door to the nurse's office opens and Dash sticks his head in. I've met Elle's brother once after school but I don't really know him. He looks like a smaller version of his sister, complete with dark hair and round eyes. He's wearing a Darth Vader T-shirt that I think Lina said something rude about one time. She's banned us from talking to younger kids. Even siblings. I'm not really sure why. Apparently they are beneath us and we have to avoid them at all cost.

"You had a party and you didn't invite me?" he says. "Thanks a lot."

"Sarah has biscuits in the staff room," says Meg, placing the last picture book on the pile.

"I can't stay. Just popped in for my emergency inhaler," he says, opening the medical supplies cupboard. "Those plane trees with their little bombs of pollen are making my throat itch. You okay?" he asks Meg.

"I'm fine, Dash," says Meg.

"She being nice?" Dash nods in my direction.

"Yes," I answer, wondering what he has against me. Maybe Lina's right. Maybe little kids are annoying.

"You'd better be," he says. "I have a posse. And an inhaler. I'm not afraid to use either!"

I laugh and he looks surprised. Then his face changes, and there's the tiniest of smiles. He steps back and lets the door shut behind him.

"Are you guys friends?" I ask Meg.

"The sort of friendship that exists only in the nurse's office," explains Meg, pulling on her slippers and getting ready to leave. "We don't talk in the schoolyard. Not really. But in here, we manage not to annoy each other. Dash and I have history. He looks out for me."

Meg's sort of skilled at mysterious conversations. She hints at more than she ever actually says. I wonder what sort of history she has with Dash.

"I really only have one friend," she says, standing up and waving the brown paper bag in the air. "I tried people, but it didn't go so well."

I watch Meg head toward the door and realize there are a hundred things I want to ask her.

She pauses in the doorway and looks around. "Isn't it nice to think that tomorrow is a new day with no mistakes in it yet?"

I have no idea what she's talking about, so I nod. "Yeah. Of course."

And with a curious smile, she's gone.

Chapter 11

MEG

"BYE, MUM," I CALL.

The house is silent. Before, at this time of the morning,
Dad would play records endlessly and Mum would hum along.
Sometimes they danced around the kitchen, dragging me into
the center, until I could escape, embarrassed by how obvious
they were. Now, the quiet has seeped into every room and my
voice is too loud.

Peggy sometimes plays records in the back room of the
laundromat while she's feeding me snacks. She often sings
along, messing up the lyrics but not caring. I wonder what
she'll have waiting for me to eat tomorrow night.

Outside on the footpath, I hurry from my house. I dodge
a silver station wagon pulling out of its driveway and walk
quickly. The weekend was hard. Mum spent most of it in bed

and I woke up this morning actually wanting to go to school. I haven't felt that way since Eleanora was my friend.

Amazingly, I arrive just as the bell rings, which is perfect timing. I'm in a swamp of hurrying people, and nobody really notices me. Just the way I like it.

Walking across the track toward the nurse's office, I spy Riley near the grade six building. I decide to change direction and stay in her shadow, walking behind. But she turns and sees me, then pauses. There's a surge in my chest when I realize she's waiting for me and, without my permission, my mouth curls into a giant smile.

I slide into position on her right, my head barely reaching her shoulder.

She looks down at me. "Hey, Meg. . . ."

"Hello, Riley . . . ," I say, unexpectedly shy, my voice like a whisper in the wind.

A soccer ball flies past my slippers and I jump back, looking around for the owner. I expect to see Lina and Matt Park laughing nearby, though nobody is watching.

"Good weekend?" she asks.

I pause, trying to find something amusing to say. "Jacked another car . . ."

She frowns and I realize she doesn't remember. It's one of my fears. That on the rare occasion when I dare to make a joke, it falls flat because the other person doesn't get it.

Then finally she smiles. "Hope it was a Mustang. A red one," she says.

"It was an RV. Big enough to live in. Something to take me away from all this," I say, waving my arms in the air.

"Why would you want to leave all this?"

"Where do I start?"

"The nurse's office, perhaps?"

I shrug. "Actually, that is the only room I like."

She stops at the steps leading to the building. There are stragglers everywhere, rushing to our grade six weekly meeting, though Riley doesn't seem to be in the same sort of hurry. I realize suddenly that I want to slow it all down so I have her even longer, and the thought scares me.

"No. There's nothing good about the nurse's office," she says. Her eyes are sparkly, like she's finding this as entertaining as I am. I force away all the flashes of fear that are flooding my head.

"Really? I love fluorescent lighting. And picture books that have been read so many times their spines are cracked. I even love the torn Healthy Eating Pyramid poster," I say lightly.

"Then it's official. You are weird," she says.

I must look surprised at her choice of words, because she opens her mouth as if to suck them back down.

"Sorry. . . . I didn't mean . . ."

"That's okay. It's true. I wear slippers to school. And I like pretending that the nurse's office is my home. I think that probably categorizes me as weird."

She looks down at my feet and taps her Converse into the

end of my slipper. Her sneakers are pale mint green and the sort I'd buy if I could.

"You aren't weird, Nurse's Office Girl," she says quietly. "No weirder than me, anyway."

When Riley smiles at me, her eyes disappear. Her face crinkles into a grin.

"Nurse's Office Girl?"

"To be honest, the whole Slipper Girl thing was my fault and I thought maybe this would be a better nickname . . . you know . . ."

I've never had a nickname before. Other than Meg, and that's just an abbreviation, not a code for friendship.

"Maybe . . . ," I tell her.

"Just saying, it's sort of my thing. Giving nicknames."

She flushes red and we stand awkwardly as students rush to put their bags away before our meeting starts. I want to ask her what it means to give me a nickname, but then I notice Lina and the others staring at us as they head into the grade six common space. Lina is shaking her head and the others are laughing. I look away quickly.

"You'd better hurry; we're late," I say, dashing up the stairs. Perhaps talking to Riley outside of the nurse's office was a mistake. I'm usually careful about showing my hand, and now everyone has witnessed it.

Because it's Monday, all of grade six has to sit in the common space for our weekly meeting.

I take my usual spot and notice that Lina's gang is sitting at a table close by. Lina is staring at me and there's nothing kind about it. I pretend to be interested in my pen. Riley must still be at her locker, because usually she'd sit with them.

"Come on, everyone, sit down, please. This morning we're discussing graduation plans," says Ms. Barber, my favorite teacher. She's younger than the others, and she has short hair and a row of piercings in her left ear. She also usually lets me work alone.

While Ms. Barber talks about all the different food possibilities for the graduation dinner, my stomach starts rumbling and I really hope nobody can hear the sound. For a second I wonder what it would feel like to care whether they served burgers, spaghetti, or tacos. Me? I'd just be happy with something that filled me up.

I hear Ms. Barber ask for volunteers to do the playlist and I watch as arms wave high into the air, straining wildly to get the teacher's attention. Finally Luca, Marco, and Lina get picked. Luca and I were friends once. I went to his birthday party when we were in kindergarten together. We haven't spoken in over a year.

Riley comes in, carrying her stuff, and I watch her realize there's no spare seat at Lina's table. She looks around to find a chair. She sees me watching her and her mouth twitches like she wants to smile but knows she shouldn't. I reach for my pocket and clutch the Bag.

"Riley, just sit anywhere for the moment," says Ms. Barber.

Riley drops a green pencil case on the floor, bends down to pick it up, then grabs it and dumps her things at the table where her friends are sitting. Tessa shuffles across and lets Riley perch on the edge of her seat. Riley looks awkward. And I'm pretty sure it's because of Lina that Riley's balancing on half of an orange plastic chair. I bet Lina's punishing her for talking to me.

"I'm handing out permission forms for the graduation dinner today. You have until the end of next week to return them," says Ms. Barber.

I hear Riley and Lina whispering about something and I'm pretty sure I hear the words "Slipper Girl." Though there is a chance I'm being totally paranoid and it actually has nothing to do with me. I risk a glance. Lina sees me looking and raises an eyebrow at Riley. I see Riley shrug one shoulder in response, like she's hanging me out to dry.

I can't believe I hoped this was different. Dash was right. This is Eleanora all over again. I clutch the corner of the Bag in my pocket, using it to calm me.

"I want everyone to fill in their preferences for graduation dinner and decorations. Quietly," says Ms. Barber, walking around and handing out a survey.

All around me chairs are dragged across the floor and

bumped as people move to sit with their friends. I'm in a group of one and I'm always quiet.

Ms. Barber heads over to me. "How's your speech going, Meg?"

Ms. Barber's been my homeroom teacher for two years. She's tried a few times to ask if everything's okay at home, and she's always very understanding if I'm feeling anxious. She even lets me work in the nurse's office sometimes.

"It's nicer to think dear, pretty thoughts and keep them in one's heart, like treasures. I don't like to have them laughed at or wondered over," I tell her.

She takes a second to answer me. "*Little Women*?"

I shake my head, disappointed. I thought Ms. Barber of all people would get it.

"*Anne of Green Gables*," I whisper.

"Of course! Sorry," she says. "Anne with an *e*. I loved those books when I was your age."

Ms. Barber leans close. "I'm pretty sure Anne would have something to say at graduation."

Sometimes even the very best adults are underwhelming. Of course Anne would have something to say because she's never short of words, but I am most definitely not Anne Shirley. For a start my hair is not red, my mother is nothing like Marilla, and I have no kindred spirit to speak of.

"Meg, I know that speaking in public is not your favorite thing, but I'd really like you to approach this as an opportunity to overcome your fears."

I've spent the past eighteen months doing everything I can to avoid people finding out about my life and now my favorite teacher wants me to stand in front of a packed gym and talk about the wonders of elementary school. "Um . . . I'm not sure that what I want to say would be appreciated on that night," I tell her.

"Meg, Mrs. Myer asked for you to speak for a reason."

Frowning, I try to understand what she's saying, although it doesn't make sense to me. Is she telling me to be honest? It doesn't really matter, because I won't be at the graduation dinner anyway.

"And, Meg, now that she's selected the boys, Mrs. Myer wants to see you all about the speeches."

"The principal?"

"Yes, the principal," says Ms. Barber, smiling.

I make a habit of not needing to speak to Mrs. Myer. So far, I've managed to keep it to a few hellos and a quick chat in seven years of primary school. I fail to see the point of starting a real conversation now.

Ms. Barber stands up and looks around the room. "Riley, Tom, and Matteo, can you go with Meg to see Mrs. Myer, please?"

There's a surge in my chest like an ambulance officer has just dropped those paddles onto me and is trying to restart my heart. I bet they did that with Dad. Charged the paddles and laid them on his chest. But there was nothing they could do. Just like Anne's father, Matthew Cuthbert.

I chance a look at Riley, who is still balancing on the edge of the chair.

"Now?" I whisper.

"Yes, Meg. Now."

The boys walk over to where I'm sitting. Tom is really tall with red hair. He's school captain and one of those kids the teachers love. Matteo's a clear choice to make a speech because he's smart and funny. And Riley makes sense because she's confident and into debating and public speaking. I'm the most unusual suspect in this lineup. Why did she choose me?

Reluctantly, I stand up, feeling a lurch in my stomach. Maybe if I vomit all over the carpet I'll escape this particular torture. I don't want to go. I really don't want to go. I snatch the Bag from my pocket and hold it up, making sure that Ms. Barber sees it. It's my "Get Out of Jail Free" card. I rarely use it in front of other students, but this is an emergency. She nods, though I can tell that the Bag is not going to be the insurance I need this time.

"Riley, can you come here, please?" Ms. Barber says.

Panicked, I look across, trying to see Riley's reaction, but all I can take in is Lina's cold stare. On the scale of bad ideas, this has to be close to the top.

"Riley, can you make sure Meg is okay?" Ms. Barber says quietly.

Riley nods but doesn't look at me. It's one thing to chat when we're alone in the nurse's office or at the shops, but I bet she hates the idea of having to be my minder in front of everyone. It's like walking through the school with a target on your back. My weird is contagious.

As we start shuffling past Lina and her friends, Lina pretends to cough and hacks out the words "Slipper Girl" just loudly enough for Riley and me to hear. The others laugh, though I don't hear Riley join in. I bet Lina won't be happy that one of her minions didn't respond.

I follow the boys down the stairs. They chatter and I stumble behind, wondering if Mrs. Myer will comment on the fact that I'm wearing slippers, and if it will become a problem for me. Safely away from the rest of the class, Riley finally walks alongside me.

"Well, this is fun," she says playfully.

I stare at her. Does she like me or not? I'm usually very skilled at avoiding situations and people where I'm made to feel vulnerable, and Riley is ruining my perfect record.

"Yeah." I need to slow my breath down. I'm gulping air in every direction. Riley touches my back and I feel her hand rubbing my skin through my T-shirt. It makes me breathe even faster. This could be a moment for the Bag to make a cameo appearance if she doesn't stop being nice.

"It'll be okay," she says.

"I'm concentrating on not having a panic attack."

"Oh . . . right," she says, obviously not knowing what to do.

"*That's* why I have this," I tell her, holding up the Bag. "It helps if I start breathing too fast."

"Oh. And it doubles as a mushroom bag," she says lightly, as if not being able to breathe is not worthy of serious attention.

We walk into the office, past Sarah sitting at her desk, and down the corridor past the nurse's office. I can't help but look across, wishing I were headed there instead. There's no sign of Dash. The room sits empty. Waiting for a witness to its crackling plastic chairs, walls, and medicine fridge. I try to veer off, but Riley's hand is back, guiding me to walk straight.

Tom knocks on the glass door of the principal's office.

"My speech team! In you come," says Mrs. Myer brightly, as we loiter in the doorway. Actually, I'm not even standing in the doorway. I'm hanging on the edge, more out than in, more fleeing than participating.

Riley stands in front of me, but she reaches back and touches my arm, like she's checking in that I'm still there. For some reason, I don't pull away. I let her fingers curl around my wrist, keeping me in place. Her hand feels strange on my skin.

"I hope your speeches are progressing nicely. It's totally up to you to write your speeches how you see fit, however, obviously, they are to mark your year's graduation from elementary school. In the past, students have spoken about their positive experiences at elementary school and their friendships and how they are looking forward to the next chapter of junior high."

I wonder if anyone else finds it interesting that we're being told we can write what we like while actually being told what to write. Then I start wondering what would happen if I wrote a really honest speech about being excluded and having no friends.

"How long should the speeches be?" asks Tom.

"No more than three minutes," says Mrs. Myer.

"And do we have to deliver them at the dinner?" Riley asks.

"Yes, that's the plan," says Mrs. Myer, explaining that she'd like to see a draft by the end of next week. Graduation is still a bit over three weeks away, so obviously Mrs. Myer is ensuring the speeches are what she wants before we have to say them.

"My door is always open for you to come and discuss your speeches. I look forward to reading them," she says.

Finally we're dismissed, and the boys race off down the corridor to return to class. I stop outside the nurse's office.

"Come on, Meg. You have to go back to class," says Riley.

My chair is calling to me from the corner. The hum of the fridge is inviting me in. Even the overhead light gives a welcoming flicker.

"In a minute," I tell Riley, walking in and sitting down in my chair.

Riley follows me. "You can't stay here forever."

"Why not?"

"Because . . ."

"That's not a reason." I glance across at the Healthy Eating Pyramid poster that I've been looking at for the last year. Every time I see it, I remember how much I want to tape down the tear across the bottom. But I never do.

"Meg . . . come on. . . ."

"You go," I tell her. "I'm staying here."

But she shakes her head at me. "Nope, we left together, we're returning together. Rules of war," she says with a smile.

And my heart cracks a little and I worry that she can hear the sound.

Chapter 12

RILEY

"HAIR, RILEY!" JENNA YELLS FROM the bathroom I share with her on the second floor.

It's Saturday and I've been dressed for Lina's party for a few hours now. Things have been a bit strange with my friends this week and I want to look perfect. I check myself in the bedroom mirror another couple of times and smile at my reflection. It's okay. My faithful black overalls hide my pump and work over the new striped T-shirt Mum let me buy online. I probably won't look as glamorous as the others, but I'm sort of used to that.

"Up in a messy bun?" Jenna says, playing with the brush.

The bathroom looks like a hairdresser's. Hair clips, ties, ribbons, and a curling iron are all laid out on the bench like she's about to operate on me.

"I don't know."

"Sit down," says Jenna.

I perch on the stool from our room and watch Jenna's reflection in the mirror. She's analyzing my head.

"You don't have lice, do you?"

"As if!" I raise an eyebrow, and she laughs at my reflection.

"You excited?"

I take a second to answer, because as much as I want to go to Lina's party, things don't feel the same as they used to with my friends. I'm not sure what's changed, exactly, but I know something has. "I still can't believe Mum's letting me go. I sort of wish I could stay all night."

She brushes my hair, pulling hard through a patch of knots. "Yeah, it's weird you're getting picked up early."

Jenna sweeps my hair onto the top of my head so my neck can be seen.

"Better than nothing," I say, trying to concentrate on the fact that I'm actually going to a party in a hotel.

"And your hair will look amazing," says Jenna. She ties my hair up in a high ponytail and then plucks strands out so they hang down, framing my face.

"Thanks for helping."

"Dad paid me," she says.

"I knew it!" Outraged, I try to stand. She grips my shoulders and pushes me back down.

"I'm kidding!"

Jenna and I don't really do hanging out together on a Saturday afternoon. In fact, this may be the longest time we've willingly spent together since she grew boobs, so I'm naturally suspicious.

"What happened to your weekend math group?"

She grins and starts fluffing out my ponytail with a comb. "It got moved to tomorrow. Aren't you lucky?"

"Do you actually learn anything?"

She shrugs. "Yeah, but it's not math related."

"Is anything you tell Mum real?"

I watch as Jenna winds my ponytail into a bun and picks up a row of pins from the bench. She smells sweet, like grape bubblegum and roses.

"She didn't always give me freedom, Riley. I know it's worse for you, but I had to lie to get out of here too," she says, then wedges the row of pins into her mouth so she can start pushing them into my hair.

She stands in front of me now so I can't watch what she's doing. I can see a line of her stomach, flat and muscled, peeping from her checked shirt that she's knotted in the front. She's always wearing little tops with jeans or shorts and big Doc Martens boots. Sometimes she knots her T-shirts up at the front after she's left the house so Mum doesn't know. She tried to show me how to do it, but it's not like anyone wants to look at a pump, so I pretended not to be interested.

I keep my hands on my knees, picking at the stitches in my overalls.

"There . . . what do you think?"

She stands to one side and meets my eyes in the mirror. I look from her face to mine, taking it all in.

"I love it," I tell her, reaching up to touch the bun.

She swats my hand away. "No touching!"

I turn from one side to the other, trying to see the back.

"Makeup?"

I shake my head, amazed that the bun doesn't move. "You're good at this!"

"Misspent youth . . ." She holds up a fat pink stick. "Lip gloss?"

I've never put anything on my face, except sunscreen. "To be honest, I don't know how to put it on."

"Pucker up," she says, moving around in front of me. She paints the lip gloss over my mouth.

"Rub your lips together," she says, showing me.

They're sticky and sweet.

"You can stop now!" she says.

I laugh and stretch past her so I can see myself. My lips look a bit shiny and pink. Just like Lina's do lately. I think she's the only girl in grade six wearing makeup to school, but if she's doing it then it won't take long for the others to start.

"Here. Take it with you," she tells me. "In case you want to reapply."

She hands me the lip gloss and I slide it into my pocket.

"Thanks, Jenna," I say, still not sure why she's being so nice.

She nods and starts sweeping all the hair accessories into

a box with her hand. Apparently, our sweet, sisterly moment has come to an end, but given that Jenna's interactions with me usually involve the rude finger and a slap across the head, today marks a definite improvement.

Six hours isn't very long when you have to squeeze in watching your friend open her presents, eating candy, painting nails, checking out the hotel gym, a movie, and dinner. The first three hours have flown by. My nails are currently green, and I've bounced on all four beds to compare the springs.

Lina has the bed in the middle. Her mum explained that it was central to the friendship group. My bed is on the end near the door because I'm not staying. When I arrived, Lina gave me a gold toiletry bag stuffed full of essentials with my name on it: an eye mask, soap, hand cream, a magazine, and some lip balm. Everyone else's also had a block of chocolate, but mine had a packet of chewing gum. Lina's mum grinned at my mum and explained that she was really onboard with the whole diabetes thing.

Mum managed to contain herself and explain the grams and what happens with a high and a low and then handed Lina's mum a laminated diabetes management plan. At least she didn't hang it around my neck like a billboard. But still, talk about embarrassing.

I was so relieved when Mum finally left. Unfortunately,

she's traded Dad, so she'll be doing pickup as well. I know it's because she wants to check on me, but she pretended she was doing Dad a favor so he could watch cricket.

Lina's mum looks like a grown-up version of Lina: same shaggy blond hair, same obsession with denim, and the same perfectly manicured nails. She's sleeping in the adjoining room, so mostly it's just been the four of us lounging around.

I've flicked through all the movies on the in-house channel about twenty million times to find something we can all agree on. We've narrowed it down to three choices: a rom-com, a Marvel movie, or a family drama.

"Shall we go for a swim first?" Lina says, leaping off her bed and flipping over into a backbend.

"Yeah!" calls Elle.

My tummy feels all jittery. "Can't we watch a movie instead?"

"No," says Lina. "The pool is gorgeous!"

"I'm getting changed!" Tessa says as she bounds up, grabs her bag, and heads for the bathroom.

I think about my promise to Mum. "I don't have my bathers," I say, pleased that I have an excuse.

Lina beams at me. "I have heaps of spares!"

"Hurry up, Tessa!" Elle bangs on the bathroom door, clutching her bathers in her hand.

Lina starts pulling everything out of her bag to show me some options.

"It's okay, L. I'll just come and watch," I tell her.

"No way! My party, my rules!" She hurls me a black bikini. "Get dressed!"

I shake my head. The bathers are skimpy and won't cover anything. I can't wear them. "Have you got anything with a bit more material?"

Lina laughs. "I didn't know you were such a prude!"

"I'm not. I just . . . They're really tiny."

Lina sighs and pulls more stuff out of her bag.

"You moving in, L?" I'm trying to lighten the moment.

"I want my party to be perfect, so I brought heaps of stuff, just in case you guys needed to borrow things. Which, obviously, you do!" She punctuates the sentence by hurling two more pairs of bathers my way.

I scoop up the dark green one-piece. "Thanks."

"Bathers were on the list of essentials, by the way. Why didn't you bring yours?" Lina looks up at me from the other side of the room.

I could tell the truth—that I had to promise Mum I wouldn't swim because swimming means disconnecting my pump and that's not something she likes me doing if she's not around. It's usually safe to disconnect for a certain amount of time, maybe ninety minutes or so, but it means lots of blood glucose checking during the swim, and also giving a bolus before I disconnect. A bolus is a dose of insulin you give on demand, unlike the basal insulin doses that are smaller and continuous and released automatically by the pump every few minutes without me having to do anything. This is the insulin I need for normal metabolism. Anyway, basically, swimming and pump disconnection is a pain. But as if I'm going to tell Lina all that.

Instead, I fake-smile, and squeak out my answer: "Forgot."

Tessa comes out in her bathers with a bath towel draped over her shoulder.

"There are striped towels poolside," says Lina, like Tessa should know better.

"Oh," says Tessa, dropping her towel on the bed.

I start to imagine how angry Mum will be when she discovers I've taken off my pump. It might mean I never get to go to another party as long as I live. I think about Meg blurting out how silly she thinks graduation is, and I wish I could be that honest. I bet Meg wouldn't put up with being bossed around by Lina, even if they were friends. In fact, I can't imagine Meg putting up with anyone. She didn't even seem scared of my mother, and usually the Brain intimidates everyone.

I decide to channel Meg. Just her attitude and not her slipper-wearing.

"L, I really can't go swimming."

Lina laughs coldly. "Why? Don't you like those bathers, either?"

"It's lovely. I just . . . It's just . . ."

"Live a little, R. You're only here for another two hours!"

Lina snatches up the bikini from my bed and strips down in front of us. She's never cared about getting changed in public.

"Come on, Riley. Your mum will understand," Tessa says gently as we both turn away and face the wall.

"Bathroom's free!" Elle shouts, chucking her clothes on the bed near us.

It's my turn.

In the bathroom, there's a large spa tub in the middle of the room that they plan to use in the morning. I strip down, take off my pump, and pull on Lina's bathers. Even these are high-cut and low-cut in all the places I'd never usually choose.

Someone bangs on the door. "Come on, R!"

I grab my things and head out into the room. They're all wrapped in big white bathrobes with white slippers on their feet.

"Sorry, R. There's no dressing gown for you," says Lina. "I guess because you aren't staying."

I nod, feeling my eyes itch as I turn away and pull on my striped T-shirt to wear down to the pool.

Elle and Tessa crowd around Lina as the three of them walk down the corridor to the lifts, chattering about breakfast the next day, and the midnight snack they plan to wake up for.

I try to catch up and squeeze in next to Tessa but the corridor is too narrow and so I trail behind. There were no slippers for me either, so I'm in my Converse with no socks on. The others look glamorous—like they belong in a Hollywood movie. I look like the extra who has crashed the party.

"When we get there, I'm going to order poolside service,"

says Lina, pressing the button for the thirty-fifth floor. "What does everyone want?"

The others start listing off a bunch of things like chips and milkshakes and soda. I just want to go back to the room and lie in bed and watch a movie. Without my pump, I shouldn't eat because I can't put grams in for food. And I've left my test kit in the room, which means I can't tell if I'm low or high.

"This way," says Lina as the lift doors slide open.

It smells like chlorine even before we reach the pool.

"Wow!" Tessa says, running ahead.

It's pretty gorgeous up here. Even though it's early evening, the sky is still blue and clear. Bunches of high-rise buildings with hundreds of windows look down into the pool, but I guess nobody is really at work on a Saturday. Just in case, I tug at my bathers, making sure they cover everything.

"It's like a Hawaiian paradise!" Elle says, running her hand along the fake grass that lines the edge of the bar. There are a few people sitting on poolside stools, but they don't seem to be aware of us at all.

"I'm going in!" Elle chucks her robe and slippers onto a pool chair and bombs into the deep end, splashing us.

I lie down on a chair, planning to take as long as I can to actually get wet.

"Come on, R," says Lina, standing over me. "Food will come up soon. But you have to swim first!"

"I'm just warming up!"

"It's about thirty degrees up here. You're stalling," she says.

I want to enjoy the party. I really do. I want to feel free and excited like Lina and the others. I just can't. I can hear the Brain's voice. *You have to take your condition seriously.*

Maybe it'll be different in the water.

There are stairs at one end of the pool that I use to lower my way into the shallow end. Elle and Tessa are having a water fight in the deep end, and Lina is next to me.

"How cool is this?" she says, sweeping her arms across the top of the water.

"Pretty cool." I take a breath. Try to clear Mum from my head.

Lina dives under and disappears into the blue. I feel her arms grab my leg and yank me down the rest of the stairs. I'm hopping, trying not to go under. I figure if I'm in for ten minutes then I can probably talk them into going back to the room.

"Let's ring your mum and tell her you're staying," says Lina, bobbing up and slicking her hair back so that it's off her face. She looks younger in the water, and I think how much she'd hate that. Ever since I've known Lina, she's wanted to look older.

"Can't," I say.

"But what's the big deal? It's not like anything will happen to you," she says.

I remember that this is what I wanted, to be here, to be allowed to be like them. But now it's happening, it's not how I thought it would feel. Sometimes I wonder if it would help Lina understand how serious it is if I caused a hyper and vomited all over her favorite sequin T-shirt. Maybe if I grossed her out enough, she'd finally get it.

I stretch up on my tiptoes so there's no risk of my hair getting wet, and try to think of a less honest answer that will satisfy Lina. Elle squeals from the other end and Tessa's legs shoot up as she does an underwater handstand.

Then Lina leaps up and out of the water, and before I can jump out of her reach, she seizes me by the shoulders and grabs me. I sort of trip my way in, and then I'm under.

Mum is going to kill me!

I quickly stand back up on the tile floor. My hair drips and sags, the bun pulling backward.

"Sorry, R," says Lina, bobbing around me on her back. "It was an accident."

But I know she's lying. She pulled me under deliberately. I turn away from her and start up the steps. I'm trying to wring all the water from my hair, but it's sopping. Elle and Tessa have joined us and the three of them bounce around me in the water. It's like they're trying to show me how much fun I should be having.

Suddenly I stop.

My hair *is* wet. It wasn't *my* fault. Maybe I could swim a little longer before getting out. I do love being in the water. It's one of the few times I can take my pump off and feel like everyone else.

I hurl myself up out of the water and splash down in the

middle of the others. Lina squeals and laughs and pushes on my shoulders, dunking me. I decide that for the next ninety minutes I'm not going to think about Mum or diabetes or anything else. I'm just going to have fun.

By the time a waiter slides a tray of food onto the table near our towels, I'm hungry. Lina swims across, clambers up the side of the pool, and signs the bill. I lie back, feeling the cool water cover me like a blanket.

"Chips, anyone?" Lina balances the plates and the milkshakes in frosted silver on the edge of the pool so we can reach them, and jumps back in.

I float, eyes closed, while the others swim across to where Lina waits. I know I can't stall forever. Lina likes it when we all participate.

Two sips. Three chips.

The strawberry milkshake that I never ordered is bright pink. The chips are crisp and salty. The others giggle as they dip in and out of the water, grabbing another handful. I slurp slowly at the sweet milk, trying to work out grams in my head so I can put them in when I go back to the room.

"Isn't this the best?" says Lina.

"I am so coming here for my party!" Tessa says.

I stop sipping the milkshake. I've had more than I meant to. I grab another few chips and slip back into the water. I know I have to get out soon, but it's so nice here. My body feels light and free. I bob, drifting slowly along the surface of the water until my feet bump the side. Behind me the others giggle and laugh and splash. The early evening sun licks my face, and I try to open my eyes but it's too bright. So I stretch out and float.

"Riley!" I can hear my name being called but I can't be bothered to stand.

Then someone grabs my arm and I dip under the water, snorting in a mouthful. I cough as I jump up. "What?"

Lina smiles at me. "Marco Polo?"

"I should probably get out," I tell her.

"No. I won't allow it. It's my birthday," she says, dropping her lip.

I blink away a furious image of the Brain when she finds out I've been swimming. "Okay."

"You're it, Tessa," yells Lina.

Tessa groans but closes her eyes as we scatter around the edges of the pool.

"No cheating, T!" shouts Lina as Tessa swims straight for her, eyes half closed.

I lean against the edge, waiting, stealing another chip from the bowl. Tessa moves fast through the water, trying to tag us all as she calls out, "Marco!" And we echo with, "Polo."

Elle's tagged first. Then Lina. Then the three of them turn on me. I swim down the middle, ducking under the water and skirting the bottom. Looking up to the surface, I see the blurry shapes of my friends hovering over me. As I come up for air, the three of them leap on me and I'm pushed under for a second.

I come up gasping for air and realize the sun is not as

bright as it was. *How long have we been up here?* As Elle starts counting, I pull the pins out of my hair and give it a shake, the movement causing my stomach to clench and swirl. I feel a bit off. My heart has a slightly racy feeling. I head for the edge of the pool.

"R?"

"Getting out," I tell her.

"But we're still playing. You are officially no fun!" Lina shouts.

"Whatever!" I shout back, wondering if maybe it's true. I need to do a test. I know I do. I grab my things, but then realize I need the key to get back to the room.

"Room key, Lina?"

Down the other end of the pool, she ignores me. I'll just knock on Lina's mum's door. She can let me in.

I head for the lift.

"Riley?" Lina calls out. "Where you going?"

I keep walking. I hit the button on the lift, leaning my head against the wall. I hate this feeling. I wonder what Meg would do if she saw me like this.

The lift doors open and I expect the others to be hurrying in behind me. But they aren't. It's just me, dripping patches of pool water onto the tile floor.

I press the button and watch the numbers dim as the lift goes down. It stops and I step out onto the blue speckled carpet, making watery footprints as I go.

I bang on the door next to our room.

It takes a minute, but then Lina's mum opens. She's dressed in a robe too. Maybe she's heading up for a swim.

"Can you let me into the other room?"

"You okay, honey?"

"Yeah. Just feeling a bit odd. Need to reconnect my pump and do a test."

As I head through her room, I'm aware of the fact that I'm wet. I hope she doesn't mind. The adjoining door is open. I discreetly strip out of Lina's bathers and pull on my clothes. I plug my pump back in and plonk down on the bed to do a test.

"I can get you a banana if you like? Low GI," says Lina's mum.

I'm sure she's trying to be kind but right now I'd like to punch her. "Thanks. Just some water." Being thirsty is a classic sign of the beginning of a high.

The machine beeps. The blood glucose reading is fourteen. I'm not too high but I need to do a correction bolus because I have high blood glucose.

Lina's mum hands me a glass of water and I drink it as fast as I can.

"More, please."

"You're dehydrated. That's not good," she says, refilling my glass.

Sometimes when I see the Hulk, she asks me for my top ten annoying comments from well-meaning nondiabetics. Lina's mum would be scoring pretty well right now. At least she hasn't tried to suggest that I've caused diabetes by eating too much sugar. That's the Hulk's personal favorite. Mine is when people ask me for jelly beans because *they're* feeling low, like it's just something that happens to all of us. I usually give them all the black ones.

I ignore her and use my pump to give myself extra insulin to correct the high blood glucose.

"You're having a hyper, aren't you?" Lina's mum says quietly from the doorway.

"We call it a high. Yeah."

"I read the sheet. Twice. If it's not a bad um, high . . . we can treat it. Right?"

"Mostly," I say, because I want her to worry for a second that maybe this won't end well. I know that's mean, but I'm feeling mean.

She nods and fills up my glass again. "It must be hard."

To be honest I'm not sure if she's talking generally about having diabetes or specifically about dashing up to the room when all my friends are still having fun in the pool. I opt for vague.

"Yeah."

As I put my glass down on the table, I see the red flashing numbers on the digital clock. Mum will be here in a bit less than an hour.

"Is there a hair dryer?" I ask in a panic.

Lina's mum nods. "In the bathroom."

I'm aware that I must appear rather odd as I jump up, then

sit back down again. "I'm not going to tell Mum I went swimming. Okay?"

I really hope Lina's mum understands what I mean. I really hope she's as keen to lie to my mum as I am. And I really hope Jenna's proud of me when I tell her that not only did I lie, I made an adult lie too.

"Why not?"

"Because swimming means I take my pump off and basically she'd kill me if she knew."

Her shocked expression makes me feel even guiltier than the lying does, except that then I remember the reason I'm wet. And it's because of her daughter, so I figure she can share the guilt.

"Okay."

I smile and disappear into the bathroom.

I'm drying my hair when the others come back from the pool. Lina's telling her mum some story about the poolside food disaster, but I can't quite hear it all over the hair dryer.

"We're going to put the movie on, R!" Lina shouts from the doorway a minute later. "Are you almost finished?"

I give Lina the thumbs-up and she leaves. It takes a bit longer to finish drying my hair but it's pretty dry. Mum would have to feel it to know that it had been in water. Now I have to try to re-create Jenna's messy bun, otherwise leaving my hair down might be a bit of a giveaway.

When I eventually come out, the three of them are lying on their beds wrapped in towels, watching the trailers. I take up position on my bed, relieved that I'm feeling better.

"You okay?" Elle asks me, still watching the screen.

"Yeah."

"Mum's ordering burgers for dinner. Are you happy with that?" Lina looks across and I know that even if I hated burgers I'd have to say yes. Besides, Mum has already worked out all the grams for me, based on an average-sized burger and a cupful of fries.

"Yum," I say.

As the movie starts, I look across at my friends, their wet hair dripping down onto their pillows.

"Wish I could stay," I tell Lina.

"Yeah. Me too," she says, staring at the screen. But her flat voice makes me wonder if it's true.

Chapter 13

MEG

MY FAVORITE PAGE TOWARD THE middle of *Anne of Green Gables* is torn slightly at the bottom. I can't remember what happened to it or when it was damaged, but each time I reach it, my thumb presses into the rip and shunts it a little higher. And, just like all the occasions I've stared at the Healthy Eating Pyramid poster in the nurse's office and had thoughts about taping up the tear, I promise myself that next time I read my well-worn book, I'll find the sticky tape in the drawer in Dad's office and repair it.

Only I don't. And I kid myself that I don't because I'm too engrossed in Anne and Diana's friendship, although actually it's because I like it damaged. I like that it needs repair. So I turn the torn page and keep reading.

In this part of the story, Anne is floating down the river in a boat pretending to be the Lady of Shalott.

I stretch out my legs, pretending my bed is a boat. The house is so quiet that I could be rocking on a river, the water lapping the sides.

I hear the door handle turn and my body tenses.

"Knock, knock, Meg," Mum says from the doorway.

I slide my book down, placing it carefully on the floor.

"I thought maybe we could walk to the shops together," Mum says quietly. "I feel quite good today and it's so beautiful outside. . . . What do you think?"

"Oh. Okay."

Mum's dressed, which means she's had a shower, and her dark hair is pulled into a ponytail low on her neck. It's been months since we ventured out.

I swing my legs out of bed, tucking them into my slippers.

"Maybe we could take a look for some shoes while we're there?"

"Yes, please," I say, looking up at her, hope radiating off me.

I fix my hair with my fingers and check myself in the tiny mirror on my desk. My freckles look darker, like they've plumped up catching glimpses of sunlight on my walks to school and to Peggy's.

At the front door, Mum pauses. I wait for her to unlock the deadbolt and gather herself, breathing deeply as she does. I wonder if she has remembered to tuck her own Bag into the pocket of her jeans. Other mothers and daughters, like Riley and her mum, might opt for matching socks or nail polish, but in our family we share a secret attachment to brown paper bags.

"Ready," she says, smiling slightly at me as she steps out of the house and into the brightness of the day.

The street is busy in that Sunday-afternoon way. A couple of younger kids I know from school have set up a stall in their front yard selling old toys. I hurry past.

Mum slips her jumper off and ties it around her waist. She stretches out her arms and I see how thin and white they are.

The shops aren't far when I'm alone, though with Mum they seem farther. Maybe because I can't daydream the way I would if she wasn't here.

"I walk this way when I go to the laundromat," I tell Mum, wanting her to know the details of my week.

"How is Peggy?"

I nod. "Her hair's blue."

Mum smiles. "The last time I saw her she'd just worked up the courage to dye a stripe at the front. It was a big deal," she says.

"No. You saw her when she had white hair," I say.

Mum looks across at me, panic flitting across her face. "Did I?"

"That time she visited when you weren't feeling . . . when you weren't well." I try to do my best to always avoid mentioning Mum's sadness. Somehow if I say the words aloud, it makes it more real.

"Oh . . . yes . . . of course."

But I know she doesn't remember. It was late last year and she'd been in bed for weeks, and I was worried because she wasn't eating much and I couldn't even drag her out for some of Peggy's minestrone. Beans and pasta soup are usually enough to make people do most things, I've found.

We reach the end of the street and I tap the button for the lights to change. The road is busy and Mum stares out like she's going to get run over.

There's a loud bang and Mum jumps next to me, letting out a tiny squeak as a hotted-up green car burns past us.

"It's okay, Mum. It just backfired," I tell her.

She touches her hair and I see her chest rapidly going up and down. "Mum?"

"I'm good."

The light changes and we start to cross. Mum is behind me. I don't dare look at her in case she changes her mind. I'm imagining buying a pair of sneakers from the shoe shop and how my life will be different when I go to school on Monday.

"Food or shoes?" I ask over my shoulder, trying to lighten everything as we walk toward the shop entrance.

She blows out a long stream of air. I hear it catch in her throat, and the gasp that comes as she looks up and sees people. Everywhere. Bustling and pushing, carrying shopping, chatting.

"Let's do food first," I tell her, heading toward the electronic doors, hoping that once she's inside she'll be okay. I power ahead and turn to speak to Mum to ask what she wants to buy, but realize she's still outside. The electronic doors have shut between us; she's out and I'm in.

I step forward to trigger the doors into opening again. The doors don't budge. I move closer and they still don't open. I step back and then forward and then back but I can't get them to slide. Then somebody walks in from the outside and the doors part, letting me rush through.

Mum is slumped up against the glass, her head bent and a brown paper bag gripped tight around her mouth. The bag fills and empties as her breathing rushes in and out.

I stand watching her. I don't know what to do. I can hear her gasping. I slide down next to her, hoping nobody from school walks past, and really hoping that Riley and her mum don't decide to do their weekly shop on a Sunday afternoon. I put my hand behind her back and rub up and down her shirt, like Sarah does for me sometimes. I can feel the bones of her ribs moving in and out below her skin.

"Mum . . . just breathe . . . slow. . . . In . . . out."

A lady slows her cart down as she wheels past, not stopping, just staring. I'd like to think that when I'm an adult I won't just hurry along pretending not to see.

The paper bag fills and shrinks with each of Mum's rapid breaths.

"Mum . . . try and hold the air in for a few seconds and then breathe it out," I tell her.

My hand keeps moving up and down her back. I lean in, smelling the crisp apple shampoo that was on sale last week when I did the shopping. Her hair falls like a screen, stopping me from seeing her face. I can just hear the bag crinkling like a pair of noisy artificial lungs.

She's had attacks like this before, but never when I've been with her in public. At home, I don't usually get this close. She tries to keep her attacks private. Like mother, like daughter.

"Mum . . . it's okay. . . ."

She nods. I take the fact she's responding as a good sign. The bag fills with air and then slowly shrivels.

"It's okay . . . ," I say again, my voice strange. I sound older, like I know what I'm doing. I move my hand away from her back and hug my legs to my stomach.

Behind us the automatic doors continue to open and close. Someone laughs. A baby squeals. A cart is returned and bumps noisily into the metal frame of another cart. And I wait for Mum to drop the bag, wondering how we ended up here.

Slowly she raises her head, her hair dropping back away from her face.

"Mum?"

She nods and I hear her swallow. Her throat is probably dry. Maybe it's sore.

"Do you need me to get you a drink?"

"No."

She turns her head, her eyes blinking. There's so much sadness reflected back at me. I look away first.

"Home?" She chokes out the word.

I nod, because I can't speak. I'm just feet away from new

shoes. Instead, I stand and reach for her arm, pulling her, helping her, lifting her until she's upright. She's still clutching the bag in one hand, like she's not quite finished with it. She lets me guide her, one arm through hers, taking slow steps like she's ancient and weak.

It's going to be a long walk home.

The nurse's office should be empty, because nobody else usually visits it this early on a Monday, but as I walk in I see that the bed is occupied by a little boy clutching an ice pack to his head. He looks up at me when I slam through the door and scurry over to my corner throne. I sit down on the cool plastic and kick off my slippers, curling my legs underneath me.

"I've got a concussion," the boy says.

"Bad luck."

"I ran into a pole," he continues.

I shrug. Today I really don't care. I start reading the medicine labels through the fridge window.

"What's wrong with you?" he says.

"My life is a perfect graveyard of buried hopes," I say dramatically, turning back to stare at him and hoping he'll stop talking. But he straightens up, dropping the ice pack and looking interested. It seems like whenever I say something intended to halt conversation, it encourages it instead. I'll definitely have to work on my delivery.

"What's that mean?"

"It means I have no friends and I wear slippers to school."

"I have lots of friends," he says. "And I'm not allowed to wear slippers to school."

"Well, good for you."

My tone makes us both frown and I know I shouldn't take things out on him. But Dash isn't here today, so the kid will have to do. For a second I wonder where Riley is and if she plans on needing the services of the nurse's office anytime soon. I decide that I'm only thinking about her because of the location and definitely not because my opinion of her has changed.

"I'll show you the egg on my head," he says, dropping his head forward.

"No," I say.

"I know why you don't have friends. You're mean," he tells me, sitting up.

I shrug, realizing he may be right. I take out a muesli bar I found in the cupboard at home. I haven't had breakfast and my stomach is growling and groaning. I unwrap it and shove the whole thing in so that the honey-covered oats mold inside my mouth and make it impossible to chew.

"You're not supposed to eat in here," he says, like he knows.

I open my mouth so he can see the mess of gooey bar.

"Yuck!" he shouts at the same moment Sarah opens the door. I close my mouth and try to swallow the gunked-up muesli.

"She's eating!"

Luckily Sarah expects me to eat in the nurse's office, given that she's usually the one feeding me. She gives me a look that says I should be more discreet and it makes me wish I hadn't taunted the boy.

"How are you feeling now, Tom?"

"Good. My egg's gone," he tells her.

"That was quick," she says.

I wonder if he really has a concussion or if he needed some quiet space too. Now I feel even worse. I've just teased a fellow classroom escapee.

"Would you like to come and press the morning bell for me, Tom?"

He nods so fast that Sarah laughs. "Bye," he says quietly as he reaches the door. He seems to have forgiven me already.

"Farewell, Tom. May we meet once more."

I force the last of the muesli bar down as Tom and Sarah leave, making the nurse's office all mine.

I only have seventeen more days of elementary school. Then I will never be able to visit the nurse's office again.

In fourteen days we have the graduation dinner. I have to show my speech to the principal by the end of the week and it's not looking great so far. I didn't have much time to work on it over the weekend, especially considering what happened with Mum. I've written a version of: *Elementary school was the best time of my life. . . . I'd like to thank my friends . . . (insert random name here) . . . my teachers . . . and wish everyone the best of luck.*

I'm not sure what to think about junior high. In some ways

I'll be more invisible. There will be more kids, so fewer people will know my business. Although, I'm not sure if they have a nurse's office and, if they do, if I'll be allowed to just hang out whenever I need.

The bell rings. Then it rings again. Unsurprisingly, it seems Tom likes pressing the button.

"There's no cake today, but I found some crackers in the cupboard," Sarah says a few minutes later as she comes back into the room.

I take the packet. It's neon orange and it's sealed. This will keep me going for the rest of the day.

"Thanks."

Usually Sarah feeds me and leaves after a quick chat, but today she perches on the edge of the bed and scoops up the ice pack that Tom dropped. I watch her long fingers knead the cold green goo inside the plastic and wait for the question that I know is coming. It takes her twenty-eight seconds. And I have to admit, I'm a little disappointed. I thought Sarah was one to get right to the point.

"Is everything okay at home, Meg?"

I wonder about telling her the truth. Then I say, "It's grand, thanks, Sarah."

"Only you've been wearing slippers for a while now and I wondered how your mum was doing."

"Oh, she's good. She's planning on going back to work. She's taking me shopping this weekend for shoes," I say, lying like a seasoned spy.

"There's nothing else going on?"

Sarah doesn't look at me when she asks this. That means she knows something is going on but can't risk my reaction. I toss up what I should say. Too many lies can get tricky and I don't want Mum getting in trouble. The last thing I want at the moment is anyone from the school having a reason to come and sniff around.

"No, no. Tomorrow is always fresh, with no mistakes in it."

Sarah frowns, causing a little V to form between her eyes. "Winnie-the-Pooh?"

"Yes, that's right," I tell her, deciding that there is no reason to stop lying now.

"Well, if you're sure, Meg?"

"Surer than sure."

Although for the first time, as Sarah gives up her attempts at uncovering the truth, I sink when she leaves.

Chapter 14

RILEY

I'M SLOW OUT OF CLASS to my locker. I haven't seen Lina and the others since the party because this morning we've been in our graduating committee groups. Now it is lunchtime and they haven't waited for me. I should do a reading before I go and find them. I look across to where I caught Meg watching me that day, but she's not there. I wonder if she's in the nurse's office and I'm tempted to go looking. Torn, I take out my lunch bag, feeling the familiar thermos shape through the padded fabric. Then I head outside.

As I walk over to the monkey bars, I see Elle and Tessa huddled around a phone and Lina cartwheeling near them.

"Hi," I say, squatting down near Tessa.

They keep watching. Elle starts giggling and Lina wiggles her way into the group and squeals. I try to lean closer so I can see what they're looking at. The screen is hard to make out from where I'm sitting. There's too much glare.

"What is it?"

"We made a movie after you left the hotel," Lina says without looking up.

"Can I see?"

"In a minute," she snaps.

"Was it fun?"

Lina pauses the movie and looks at me. Tessa and Elle join her and I realize the three of them are wearing the same frosted-pink lip gloss.

"Yeah. Course."

I nod. "Good. That's good."

"The breakfast was amazing! You would have loved it. No pumpkin soup to be seen," says Elle.

I smile at my friend, pleased she's at least making an effort to include me.

"We got busted waking up for a midnight feast," says Tessa with a giggle. "But Lina's mum couldn't stay mad for long and told us to eat quietly!"

"Then we went shopping all day in the city," says Lina.

"Oh," I say, wondering why they didn't at least invite me.

"We bought our graduation dresses," adds Lina. "*We're* all wearing navy."

I notice the emphasis on *we*, like I'm no longer part of it. I nod, then wonder why I'm nodding. "Sorry I had to go home."

Lina shrugs like she doesn't care. "Used to you not being there, R."

I swallow, wishing it wasn't true, wishing I wasn't the one who never came. At least Mum didn't find out I'd been swimming. I had to admit to the high, and that meant a short lecture about carbohydrates, but she was pleased that I'd corrected it and done all the right things.

Lina turns her focus back to her phone and presses play. I sit back against the monkey bars, sipping my soup, while my friends giggle over something I can't see. I bite down on my lip as the playground buzz fills my ears, and I feel like the only quiet thing here. Now I'm wishing that instead of coming out here, I went to the nurse's office. Meg might wear slippers to school, but she doesn't make me feel like this.

I tune back in to my friends in time to hear them making plans to go shopping on the weekend for matching shoes to wear with their dresses.

"You should come, R," says Tessa.

"She won't be allowed," says Lina, helping herself to a handful of crackers from Elle's lunch box. "Will you?"

"Maybe," I say, blinking away the scratchy feeling in my eyes.

"There are no parentals coming," she says, like that will seal it, and then she smiles at me.

"I think we're busy on the weekend, anyway," I say, knowing that nobody believes me.

"See? Told you," Lina says to the others.

Tessa smiles at me. It's kind but unhelpful. Elle shakes the box of crackers in my direction and I take one because there's nobody around telling me not to.

"Can't believe they chose that group of creeps to make graduation speeches," says Lina. "No offense, R."

I shove the cracker into my mouth so that I can concentrate on chewing it.

"Yeah, I know. Can't believe Slipper Girl gets to speak," says Tessa.

"What's she going to say? It's not like she has any friends!" Elle adds.

I steal another cracker from Elle's lunch box, wishing the bell would ring, wishing the tree would fall down, wishing that aliens would land and beam me up. Anything to derail this conversation.

"Didn't you used to be her friend, Elle?" asks Tessa, drawing out her words like Lina does.

"They were besties, weren't you, Elle?" adds Lina.

Elle shakes her head and fidgets with the lid on her lunch box. "In grade four."

I look over at Lina, wondering where this is going.

Lina smiles. "But then I saved you."

Suddenly the missing pieces click into place. Elle was Meg's friend. Dash is Elle's little brother. That's why Dash and Meg have history.

"What sort of dress are you going to buy?" Elle asks me.

"You'll need something baggy so it doesn't show your pump. Don't want everyone thinking you're fat!" Lina says, smiling at me like I'm supposed to laugh.

"Nice, Lina!" My voice is softer than I'd like.

"Calm down. As if I'm being serious," she says, rolling her eyes at the others. "Maybe you're having a low. Have you done a test? You're a bit cranky."

I clamp my jaw as tight as I can and count silently to five so I don't explode. This is worse than an argument with mum. I'm really not sure what's going on.

Suddenly Lina pushes me out of the way so she can see over my shoulder. "Look! Slipper Girl's taken Matt's soccer ball," she says, standing up.

It looks like Meg's arguing with Nick Zarro and Matt Park, and I want to cheer her on. Those boys think they own the track and the girls can either watch or stay out of their way. But I wonder what happened to make Meg grab the ball in the first place.

Nick reaches out for the ball and tries to wrestle it from her. Meg's not letting go.

Lina tosses her apple onto the ground and starts running over to where they're arguing. Tessa and Elle follow. They're like ants all in a line, scurrying to the crumbs.

I stand up and hurry after them too.

"What's your problem, Meg?" I hear Lina call out.

Meg looks at the ground, the ball tucked under her arm. I wonder where the yard-duty teachers are and why they haven't swooped in on this and shut it down.

Lina walks super close to Meg. "Can you hear me, Slipper Girl?" Lina shouts.

Tessa laughs, and Nick and Matt join in.

"Apparently, I kicked it too close to her legs . . . so she took it," says Matt.

Lina grins at him. I can feel the energy in the air changing. "Maybe she was worried her slippers would get dirty. Oops, dirtier!"

Matt laughs and Lina straightens at the sound, like she's inflating.

"It's not very nice to take things that aren't yours, Slipper Girl," says Lina, reaching around behind Meg and punching the ball, knocking it up and out of her arms.

Surprised, Meg looks around, and I see her notice me. Nick scoops up the ball from the ground and kicks it long, back toward the track. He grins at me like I should be impressed and I look away like I'm not.

The boys run off, heading after the bright orange soccer ball, like it's a beacon. I'm pretty happy to see them go, but now I'm left with my friends who don't seem to be done with Meg yet.

"So, what's with the slippers?" Lina says, leaning in even closer so her nose is nearly touching Meg's cheek.

I see Meg stiffen. Elle flicks a glance my way like she's not sure what to do, but Tessa is already copying everything Lina's doing.

"Come on, let's go finish lunch," I say to my friends, hoping my power still holds.

"We're going to finish this first," says Lina.

She kicks at Meg's feet, covering her slippers in brown dust. I hear Meg take a breath and another one. She's staring at the ground like she wants it to suck her down and spit her out someplace else.

"What's with the slippers, Meg? Tell us," says Lina.

"Yeah, tell us, Slipper Girl," echoes Tessa.

Meg steps back, trying to break the circle and move away, but Lina and Tessa move around behind her.

"Move," says Meg. Her voice sounds shaky and strange.

"She speaks!"

This time both Tessa and Elle laugh at Lina's joke.

"Why do you always wear the same clothes?" Lina asks, smiling at us like this is fun.

I grab for Lina's arm, trying to make my voice light and loose. "Come on, guys. Enough."

I take a step away, hoping that if I leave, my friends will forget about Meg and come too. But Lina and Tessa seem locked into something.

I see Meg pull a crumpled paper bag from her pocket and hold it up to her face. She sucks at the bag and Lina laughs loudly. I know what that is. Meg's having a panic attack.

"Okay, leave her alone now, Lina," I say, more firmly than before.

Lina spins around and turns her attention to me. "You taking her side?"

"Just leave it, Lina," I say again, feeling my heart race and wondering if it's the low or just the argument. "You okay, Meg?" I say.

Meg's eyes find mine over the edge of the paper bag. Then she turns away from us and runs, like a bird with a broken wing, straight toward the admin building.

"What was that about, Riley?"

Lina is facing me with her jaw set and her braces gleaming. I've seen her in attack mode before but it's never been aimed at me.

"I just didn't want anything to happen to Meg. She's nice."

Lina gives me her best fake smile, usually reserved for our teachers. "Obviously, you don't really want to hang with us anymore. Maybe you like Slipper Girl more."

I shake my head. "What are you talking about?"

She raises an eyebrow and my heart races. "You can never do anything we do. You're always rushing off. Making excuses. Clearly, you're not that into us."

I'm aware of Tessa and Elle watching me, waiting to see whether to leap in or not.

"I am. I came to your party. You're my friends. . . ." My words sound thin and weak.

Lina shrugs and a smile transforms her face. I try to relax but my shoulders are up too high, tense and uncomfortable.

"Prove it."

"How?"

She grins at me. "You'll see."

"Okay." I nod too much.

"O-kay," says Lina, drawing out the word. "I'm going to chat with Matt now."

The three of us watch as she heads across to where the boys play soccer. Halfway over she flips a perfect cartwheel, lands on her feet, then straightens up and keeps walking. I wait for Elle or Tessa to say something, anything, but they're both as still as I am, like we've all just been extras in a film scene that we weren't expecting.

"Toilet," I tell my friends.

Elle waves her hand but they don't look up as I leave. They're too busy watching Lina.

"Riley?" Sarah looks up from behind her computer as I pass Reception.

"Just grabbing a Band-Aid for my finger," I tell her, pushing open the door and hoping to find Meg. Instead, Dash is reading a comic in the other chair.

"Hi, Dash," I say.

He nods, his dark hair flopping down. "Riley," he says,

holding up an inhaler. He pushes his hair out of his face and starts shaking his inhaler from side to side.

"Have you seen Meg?"

He shakes his head and then makes an elaborate show of checking under the bed and in the corner of the room. "Nope, sorry."

"Thanks," I say, heading for the door.

"Thought you needed a Band-Aid," he says.

"I did."

"She's not like you or your friends. Maybe you should leave her," he says.

I turn back to him, frowning. "What do you mean? You don't even know me!"

I'm used to being judged before people know me. Judged because of the whole diabetes thing, not because of who my friends are. Or who I am. I don't like that at all.

"You're friends with Lina, right? Meg is a target to people like her. Don't make it harder for Meg by drawing attention to her."

"You've known Meg for ages, right? Because of her and Elle?"

"Yeah . . . ," he says testily.

"What happened with them?"

Dash leans back in the chair like he's trying to work out whose side I'm on. "They were best friends since preschool. Then my sister dumped Meg for Lina."

"But that stuff happens all the time. . . ." I know I sound desperate, but we're talking about my friends.

Dash raises one eyebrow and it reminds me of something Meg would do. It makes me question how I feel about everything. How I feel about my friends.

"Are you Meg's friend?" I ask him.

"I understand her," he says. "And I like her."

I'm not sure what to say. He smiles at me but it's a full stop, not an invitation for more conversation. Then he picks up his comic and starts reading, leaving me hanging by the door, feeling like I don't belong anywhere, and I'm not sure what to do with that.

"Band-Aids are in the cupboard," says Dash.

"My finger's healed," I tell him.

"It's a miracle," he says, not bothering to look up.

Chapter 15

MEG

HEADING AWAY FROM THE GATE, I look back once, just to make sure no one has followed me. The schoolyard is quiet. Everyone else is safely restored to their classrooms, and except for the odd piece of forgotten fruit and discarded sandwich wrappers, the grounds are empty.

I've never skipped out of school before. That's what the nurse's office is for. But I didn't want to talk to Riley if she came looking for me, so here I am, rushing away with an empty bag on my shoulder like I have somewhere to be.

I'm concentrating on not thinking about Riley. It takes so much energy to not think about someone. Though not thinking about someone is easier when they aren't right in front of you. I should know. I've done it for years. I've watched Mum and tried to not to think about her at the same time. I'm very practiced at it, but still I find it hard.

In a couple of hours this sidewalk will be packed with parents hurrying to pick up their kids. Mum used to do that when I first started school. She'd arrive early and wait near the classroom, making small talk with the other parents. I'd come out and she'd wrap me in her special after-school hug, kiss the top of my head, and hand me a snack. Now some days I doubt she even remembers I'm in grade six. I may as well have died back when Dad did.

I stop in at home for my dirty laundry and find Mum in bed. She's lying in the dark, so I don't bother disturbing her. I just pile up as much as I can fit in my schoolbag and head off to see Peggy.

I walk around the corner and see a flash of pink through the window. Peggy looks like she's rolled her head in cotton candy. I stare in, watching her fold towels into neat squares and place them into a giant basket. She smooths the top of each one, her blue-painted nails flashing in the light as she moves. She's wearing a checked red-and-white shirt tucked into high-waisted jeans, and she looks like an actress out of a movie.

"You're pink!"

"You're a day early," she says, raising an eyebrow like she's trying to work something out. "Actually, you're more than a day early. School hasn't even finished yet."

She drops the towel she's folding back into the basket and walks over to wrap me in a detergent-smelling hug. Peggy always smells like washing powder.

"We were let out early. Curriculum half day," I tell her, avoiding her eyes.

"Lucky you. Wish I could finish early," she says with a smile. "Do you like my hair?"

"Yes. Can you dye mine?" I ask.

"No. You're twelve! Your mother would kill me. How is she, by the way?"

I consider my words while the machines hum and vibrate through the floorboards, calming me. The air is swampy and thick, but I like it. It always feels like a blanket that trails around, keeping me safe.

"Recovering. I do believe she's considering going back to work."

"That's huge, Meg."

I shrug, turning away before she can read my face, but there's nothing in what I've said that isn't true. I'm sure Mum is considering going back to work; it's just that she'll probably consider that it's too hard.

"I knew she'd get there. Grief takes time, honey," she says, sliding my backpack from my shoulders. "Number four's empty. And here's a top to put on so you can wash Gumby," she says, handing me a green T-shirt with a rainbow on it.

I dash out the back to change. The T-shirt is so soft that it's almost transparent; like it's been washed so many times, it's barely holding together. It smells like lemons. I slip it on, liking how the sleeves flop down to my elbows.

"Grab a biscuit while you're there!" Peggy calls to me like she can read my thoughts. "There's some in the tin. I haven't quite finished the lasagna, because I thought you'd be here tomorrow!"

I snatch a couple of biscuits with chocolate piped in perfect lines across the top from Peggy's favorite vintage cake tin. I hold them in my warm hand, feeling the chocolate press into my skin. Then I shove one after another into my mouth and lick my palm.

Mum disappears with the first biscuit, and Lina with the second. I try to make Riley vanish too, although I doubt even eating the entire tin of biscuits would keep her out of my head.

"That green's a great color on you," says Peggy, looking up from folding sheets when I walk over to the machine.

I toss Gumby and the rest of the washing in and sprinkle the good powder across the lot. There are barely enough clothes for half a load. I turn the dial, causing the water to start flooding in.

"Meg? Did you hear me?"

"What?"

I look over and see concern on Peggy's face. I try to find a smile.

"You okay?" she asks, putting down the sheets and moving closer.

"I'm so glad I live in a world where there are Octobers," I say, hoping the quote will lighten the mood.

"It's December tomorrow," says Peggy, rubbing her hand through her pink hair.

"Well, yes, although the quote doesn't work quite so well if I make it accurate," I tell her.

"You're shaking, honey," she says, touching me.

I swallow, but crumbs from a biscuit rise in my throat. As Peggy's arms wrap around my middle, I begin to come unstuck. There's a shudder from my feet up my body, and a sob erupts from my throat before I can silence it.

Peggy pulls me in even closer so I can feel her ribs and her strong arms circling me and it's all I need to start crying and hiccupping and sobbing all over her. Everything pours out in a snotty mess. Each time one wave ends, another starts. Until I've emptied it all.

"Come on, let's go out the back," she says, leading me around the laundromat. First she slides the lock up and turns the sign that says she'll be back in five, and then she guides me out through the door into the back room.

She places me down onto a chair and starts making tea. I wipe my eyes with both palms, then give up and just hold the green T-shirt over my face.

"Lucky I own a laundromat. Two sugars today," she says, spooning it into my cup.

"Sorry," I tell her.

"What for?"

I shrug and stare at the floor, focusing on the cracks and scratches.

"Meg, it's okay," she says, reaching over and touching my hand.

But it's not. I don't tell. I keep it hidden. I'm slipping. This isn't good. This is Riley's fault. She started scratching at the edges and unpicked my scabs and now I'm oozing in public.

I roll my shoulders and feel a tug as the muscle stretches down the middle of my back. Everything's stiff. Everything hurts.

"I'd better go," I say, standing up.

Peggy places both hands on my shoulders. I feel them kneading into my skin. "Sit down," she says, forcing me back into the chair.

I say nothing as the kettle screams behind her and she turns away to fill the teapot with water. I could make a run for it. But she reaches across for my hand. I let her take it. I let her squeeze it between her warm palms. She holds on, just waiting for me to be ready.

I reach for a biscuit, but stop. It doesn't seem right to be eating at the moment. Peggy must sense how I feel because she pushes the tin toward me along with my tea. This time I take a biscuit and start nibbling around the edge.

"What's happened? Is it your mum?" says Peggy quietly.

I look up at her. Her eyes are so soft and concerned.

It's all too much. I jump up and knock the cup of tea, spilling it everywhere. I can't be here.

"Meg . . ."

She chases after me, but I'm faster than her. As I bound out onto the street, I realize all my washing is still churning and turning in the big steel drum of Peggy's machine.

The front room doesn't take long to vacuum and tidy up. I like keeping this room neat. Nobody really uses it much anymore, although if I need to feel close to Dad, this is where I come. He built the bookshelves that line the walls. They're made of thick slabs of red gum he had left over from a building site. It was our story room, Dad and me. We'd curl up in front of the heater and I could pick any story I wanted from the library in his head, and we'd snuggle up and he'd put on funny voices as he talked.

I punch the cushions and rearrange them on the couch and then draw the curtains so that the room looks used. The sunlight stripes through the window and casts tree shadows on the furniture. The room might be tidy but it still doesn't look like it has any life. I dash out the back into the yard to the magnolia tree that has just started flowering. I reach up and grab a branch with four bulbous pink-and-white flowers getting ready to spread their petals, and bend the branch halfway down. It takes a few goes back and forth until it snaps and then I carry it carefully back into the house.

The magnolias look out of place in the front room. Like they're trying to show off and aren't quite capable of dragging the rest of the place up to their standards. I wonder if I should move them.

"Meg?"

Mum is in the doorway wearing her old paint-splattered T-shirt. It swamps her entirely, draping down to her knees. "It looks lovely in here. Thanks for cleaning up."

I risk a nod.

"New T-shirt?"

I look down. The rainbow is stretched in colored lines across my chest. I hope Peggy didn't expect it back. Mum walks into the room and I watch her closely. She stands in front of the couch for a second, and then slowly sits down, like she's trying it out. She pats the seat next to her. I'm slow to join her and when I do, I leave a cushion width between us.

"How's school?"

"Fine."

"I did some gardening today . . . weeding. I pulled out weeds," she says, holding out her hands like I should be able to see the evidence. "It was gorgeous outside. The days are getting warmer," she says.

I notice the pink in her cheeks. She's usually so pale. Today must have been a better day. If only there was a row of better days before the bad days come.

"Thought I'd cook something tonight. Do you feel like pasta? There's basil in the garden," she says.

I don't want to be fooled; I've rushed into these moments before.

Through the window, I see Peggy walking along the footpath

with a basket of washing. I catch her eye as she passes and shake my head firmly, hoping she understands, but she keeps coming.

"Meg?" Mum asks.

I'm staring out, the sun beaming in, knowing that any second, there will be a knock or a doorbell ring or something. My left knee starts shaking, vibrating, like it's getting ready to run.

"It's Peggy," I whisper.

"What?"

"Outside," I tell her, snatching a quick look at her face as she processes the information.

The knock is quiet when it comes, like she knows it will be met with fear.

Mum gasps and drops her head, looking at the ground.

"It's okay, Mum."

Leaving her, I go to the door.

"Your washing, madam," says Peggy, holding out the basket to me, the smell of detergent strangely reassuring. I slide my hands into the rope handles, and notice that she's pressed and folded each piece. And on top is a large orange Tupperware container that I'm guessing is full of lasagna.

"Your mum home?"

I shake my head. "No."

"Can I come in?" She starts edging toward the doorway, but I hold my ground, blocking her with the laundry. There's a cough from inside the house like someone's being choked.

Peggy scans my face and then places her hands on my shoulders and turns me to the side so she can pass.

She heads straight for the front room, shutting the door behind her as she goes inside, leaving me in the hallway with the washing.

At first I pace. Up and down the hallway. Then I stand outside the closed door with my head pressed against it, trying to listen. I can hear crying and voices, though nothing specific. *What is going on in there?* Last time Peggy came, Mum told her to leave and never come back and, afterward, Mum was in bed for a week. Nothing is worth triggering that. Not even a tub of cheesy, saucy lasagna that I'd happily eat cold.

It wasn't like this after Dad died. Not straightaway. She worked and I went to school and at night I'd creep in and slip into Dad's side of the bed and wake up wrapped in Mum. But then she stopped talking about him, stopped getting up in the morning, and started sleeping on her side, away from me. And I didn't know what to do. Soon after that I saw her use a paper bag for the first time, her breathing fast and choking, and her face stained with tears.

It was his heart. His big, sweet heart. It just stopped one day on a building site and his friend called an ambulance, but it was too late.

I think that's what got to her. The speed of it. The here one day, gone the next. Instead of healing with time, her grief just grew and grew until it settled somewhere inside.

I feel it too, the pain of him never coming back. I understand why she's like this. Although unlike her, I try to remember him. His hands, measured up against mine, swamping me. His laugh that started somewhere down deep and shook his body. And that he smelled like wood. He'd shake his hair and shavings would fall from it like snow. He'd take off his boots and a small splinter would drop. Peggy told me once he could read the grain. He could run his hands down a timber beam and know how it would react. I always loved that idea.

I miss Dad. I do. But I miss Mum more.

What is going on in there?

Chapter 16

RILEY

"HERE'S YOUR SNACK, RILEY," SAYS Jess, the aftercare worker.

I take the package wrapped in foil. Everyone else gets to line up in a long, snaking queue across the middle of the playground and choose whichever slices of jam-covered bread they feel like. Me? I have twenty grams of specially prepared snackage. I should do a test before I eat the crackers, just to check I'm not low or high.

But instead, I decide to sit down on the edge of the wooden steps and wait for Lina. I'm only here on Wednesday afternoons and Lina is almost never here. There are kids everywhere. Some are kicking balls and others are chasing each other around the school.

"Apricot jam is so underrated, don't you think?" She stands

in front of me, squishing together the two slices she's holding, and takes a big bite.

"I wouldn't know. I have Vegemite. The only spread with zero grams."

I show her the rice crackers smeared with the thick brown paste. Not even any butter.

"Yummy . . . Lucky, R." She sits down next to me, her leg squashing against mine. "Eat up, R," she says, stuffing in the last of her sandwich.

"Why? You want to play soccer with the grade twos?"

She shakes her head at me and I see a shine of something in her eyes that I can't quite pin down. "We're getting out of here."

"What do you mean?" Lina's only here because I am. Her mum doesn't care if she walks home to an empty house. She has her own key and money to buy snacks on the way. She told me this morning that she'd asked her mum to book her in to a casual session for tonight, but she never told me why.

"Time for you to have some fun."

The dry Vegemite cracker wedges in my throat and I cough to free it. I'm suddenly not very hungry.

She grabs my arm and pulls me up. "I'll meet you round near the back of the library. Leave your stuff. We have to come back. What time's your mum coming?"

"Lina . . . I can't . . ."

She sighs and rolls her eyes. "Yeah, you can. This is what friends do. What time's your mum coming?"

I shrug. "I dunno. Five thirty . . . six."

"Cool. We've got nearly two hours."

She runs off toward the gym. I know she used to skip out of aftercare before her mum said she could walk home, but this is the first time she's asked me to do it too. If Mum finds out then I'm dead. No, I'm definitely worse than dead. Plus, I'm not even sure I want to skip out of school. But if I don't go, Lina will never let me forget it. She holds on to everything. And maybe this is a chance to show her that I can do things. I toss the last bits of my rice crackers into the bin and head off after her.

There's a small gap between the back of the library building and the fence, and it's planted with bushes and trees. I can see Lina huddled behind them when I round the corner. My hands are clammy, and I can't stop looping the thought of being caught through my head.

"I'll jump the fence first. Okay?" she whispers.

"Okay."

I watch as she puts her hands out and springs over the rail, doing a handstand at the top, like it's a gym routine.

I squeeze through the bushes, feeling the scratch of the twigs and sharp leaves on my bare arms. There's so much rubbish on the ground. It's like everyone comes here at lunch and dumps half-eaten sandwiches and apple cores. I reach the part of the fence where Lina climbed over.

"Hurry, R," she says.

I sling my leg over and haul myself up and over the thin

metal. I look around to make sure nobody's seen us but every-one is on the track or in the art room or kitchen. You're not supposed to come down here during aftercare and I guess they figure if you've signed in, it's unlikely that you'll do a runner. I throw myself clear of the fence and land clumsily near Lina.

"Where are we going?"

"You'll see." Lina pulls her phone out of her pocket. We're supposed to hand our phones in at aftercare but somehow she always manages to fool Jess that she's left it at home that day. Lina never surrenders her phone. It's always in her pocket, like she needs it to stay alive.

I watch her text and try to read over her shoulder, but she keeps it just slightly out of sight so I can't. "Lina?"

She pockets her phone and strides ahead. I skip to keep up, worrying that this is not a good idea. I never really walk any-where without Mum or Dad. Someone is bound to see me leave school. Or maybe Jess will go to check on me and they won't be able to find me at school and they'll call Mum. My palms are itchy, and I flick my nails across them, hoping to scratch the feel-ing away.

"How much farther?"

"Why? Don't you trust me?"

Lina checks the traffic at the roundabout and heads across, pausing in the middle to let a bike go. I follow and we pass a row of identical-looking gray houses. I wonder how far we're going.

"Let's cross here," Lina says, reaching the end of the street.

We walk down another street that looks the same as the last

one. I've only lived here for eighteen months and I have no idea where I am. If I had to find my way back to school it would be disastrous. Lina bumps against me as we near the corner of the main road. She turns left and I follow.

"You going to tell me where we're going?"

She looks across and grins. "Almost there, R."

I roll my eyes, pretending not to care, but inside my stomach is churning like it does when I haven't eaten properly.

"Mum said I could get a limo for graduation and pick us all up. What do you think?" she asks.

I think my mum will have something to say about that, but I nod and try to animate my face. "Amazing."

"I know. I'm so lucky. She's letting me get my makeup done so that it stays on for the after-party. Mum might be super busy but she totally gets what I'm into."

I think about my mum and how little she gets what I'm into.

"Mum's going overseas next week, so she won't be at graduation," adds Lina. Her mum is away a lot. It means she has to stay with her dad and his new family, whom Lina doesn't get along with.

"She might even miss Christmas," whispers Lina, her head down.

"Oh. That sucks." I touch her arm, trying to be supportive, and she lets me for about ten seconds before she pulls away and shrugs.

"Yeah, but imagine the presents I'll get when she comes back. A-mazing!"

Lina skips across the road in front of a car. I wait until it cruises past before following after her.

"So, what's with you and Slipper Girl, then?"

"Nothing."

Lina pins me with one of her famous *As if* looks, complete with an eyebrow up in judgment. I tried to master this look, but after an hour of practicing in the mirror it was obvious I had nothing on her.

"TBH, she's okay," I finally say.

"Bonded in the nurse's office, have we? Nice," she says coldly. "She's probably delighted to have some attention."

"Why do you hate her so much?"

She shrugs. "It's just a bit of fun, R."

Before I moved here, "fun" meant a rollercoaster ride, or a sleepover at my house, or climbing a tree. I'm not sure I like this new definition.

I look up and see a boy waving at us from about one hundred meters away.

"Is that Matt Park?"

Lina turns and smiles at me. "Sure is."

"We're meeting Matt?" I say, realizing I've just been dragged from aftercare for a boy.

"And Nick."

I groan. "No, Lina. I don't like Nick."

"I couldn't meet them on my own, could I? I needed a bestie," she tells me, slipping her arm through mine and pulling me closer to the boys.

I'm not sure whether I feel angry with her or relieved that she just called me her bestie.

"And you get to have your first-ever Slurpee! My treat," she says, as we reach the boys and I notice that they're waiting outside the 7-Eleven for us.

"Hey," I mumble to Nick.

He mumbles back at me while Matt and Lina start giggling about something. I really wish I'd stayed at aftercare.

"Riley's never had a Slurpee before. Let's show her how it's done," she says, pushing the door open and waving the three of us in.

Matt bangs in before me but Nick stands back so I can go next. This is so awkward.

"Thanks," I say.

"Yep."

Inside the store is bright and busy. I'm trying to imagine what Mum would be angrier about—me ducking out of aftercare, meeting a boy, or having a Slurpee. I can't decide. Probably all three. Hopefully she'll never find out, just like she never found out about the swimming.

Lina hands me a giant cup. "Slurpee initiation begins!"

Nick shuffles closer and talks me through the available flavors—Coke, Fanta, and raspberry—and then shows me how to hold the cup up to the nozzle and turn it on. I'm madly trying to calculate the grams as a stream of bright pink icy goo pours out and starts filling the cup.

Matt flicks the tap off halfway. "You gotta get all three flavors."

"Okay."

"I'm not drinking Coke," Lina says loudly. "It'll rot your teeth." Then she laughs like she's hilarious and bumps Matt along so she can fill her cup with the stream of icy Coke.

"Here, Riley," says Nick. "You need a straw-spoon thing."

He pushes the paper down from the outside of a straw and hands it to me. My cheeks are probably as red as the Slurpee, and I start drinking because I don't know what else to do.

"Go slow. You'll get a brain freeze!"

"Oh. Okay." I sip slowly, knowing I have to do a test and put in grams. But how much of this is soft drink and how much is air? I know that soft drinks are packed full of sugar, which means carbohydrates.

As Lina turns around to go to the counter and pay, I lean in and whisper, "How many grams do you think this would have?"

She pulls a face at me and starts sucking on the straw. "I dunno!"

"But I have to put the grams into my pump," I say, louder than I mean to.

"Live a little, R!"

Nick looks over and I can see him trying to work out what's going on. Embarrassed, I turn away. I don't want to have a conversation about diabetes with him or Matt.

I decide to sip as slowly as I can. It should be okay. It has to be okay. It was okay when I went swimming and that was exercise *and* a milkshake and chips. This is just flavored air and a bit of ice. I try to breath normally as Lina pays and the boys crash into the street with their Slurpees.

"Let's go to the park," says Lina.

"What's the time? I have to be back soon," I say nervously.

"Yeah, yeah . . . plenty of time."

Lina walks up to Matt and they head toward the traffic lights. I can see the big park across the road. I know it's not far from school because we walked to it for interschool sports this year.

"What's your favorite flavor?" Nick asks.

"Um . . . I dunno."

"I like Fanta. All that orange."

"Yeah."

We walk next to each other but both of us are looking down like our Slurpees are fascinating. I have to ask him a question to break the silence, but I don't know what to start with. After a few moments, I say, "Are you excited about graduation?"

"I guess. The after-party's supposed to be fun."

"Yeah."

The lights change and we keep walking, Matt and Lina yards in front. I can hear Lina's voice chatting away and I wonder what she's finding so easy to talk about.

"You excited?" he asks.

I sip a bit more Slurpee but can't work out what flavor is what. It all just tastes sweet and cold.

"Yeah. I have to do a speech."

"Bummer."

"Yeah." I blink a couple of times, trying to shift the sharpness in my head. "I think I have a brain freeze!"

"My dad says you should punch your head . . . like this." I look across as Nick bangs the flat part of his palm against his forehead. His eyes close as he does it, and it makes me laugh.

"No thanks!"

"It doesn't work," he says. "Probably makes it worse."

"Yeah. I reckon." I take another sip and realize I've drunk more than I meant to, but it tastes delicious.

"Over here, R!"

Lina's sitting on the swing at the playground and Matt is on the ground at her feet. I follow Nick across to them.

"Slurpee verdict?" Lina asks me.

"Yeah . . . good."

"Told you! You were missing out. Such a drag being diabetic," she says.

Blushing, I focus on my Slurpee and wonder what Lina is playing at.

"So, should you not have sugar?" Nick asks.

"It's fine," I tell him.

He nods and I really hope he stops with the questions. I hate talking about diabetes like it's a public forum.

I'm getting anxious about putting grams into my pump. I have to do a test first, because if I put in grams without knowing what my reading is, I could cause a low or a high. Then I realize I didn't even test before I had half the crackers at aftercare. It's always a risk if you eat without testing because you don't know what your blood glucose level is and then you're adding more food to it. It makes it impossible to know how many grams to put in. But there is no way I'm going to test in front of the others. I scan the park looking for a toilet, but I can't see one anywhere. There are just joggers and kids on bikes and more seagulls than I've ever seen away from the beach.

"I should probably head back to school," I say, deciding I can wait and do a test there.

Lina scoots her feet along the ground, making the swing rock gently so she can bump into Matt. "We have heaps of time."

"Yeah, but what if Mum's early?"

Lina rolls her eyes at me. "Stop being so boring!"

I frown. I hate it when Lina gets like this. "If I'm late back . . ."

"Yeah, I know. You'll get in heaps of trouble!" she says in a silly voice.

Matt and Nick both laugh and I look down at the ground, clutching my Slurpee and chewing on the straw.

"I can just go back on my own. It's fine. Tell me the directions," I tell her.

Midswing, Lina jumps off and lands on her feet. "Maybe Nick can walk you?"

She looks behind me to where Nick is leaning against the swing set. "Whatcha reckon, Nick?"

I shake my head at her. I know she wants to get rid of us both, but I don't want this. She grins at me, turning away from the boys so they can't see her expression.

"Sure . . . ," says Nick.

"All sorted, then," Lina says, slurping up the last of her drink and crushing the cup in her hand.

Angry, I start heading out of the park, scuffing my Converse through the sticks and dirt on the ground. I figure Nick will catch up but to be honest I'm done worrying about any of them.

"Wrong way, R!" Lina shouts with a laugh.

My heart is gathering itself too fast. I need to go to the toilet and I don't want to make small talk with Nick Zarro.

"This way," says Nick, catching up with me.

Feeling my cheeks flush even more, I follow Nick across the road.

We walk around the corner toward the back of the library. I don't feel very well and I just want to get back and check my blood glucose levels before Mum arrives. I've stopped talking because I'm concentrating on my feet. Nick's not talking either, so it's a pretty awkward walk. I'm going to kill Lina when I next see her.

I can hear the sounds of kids playing at aftercare. I'm really thirsty, and I'm hoping it's just because we've walked fast in the sun, and not because it's the beginning of a high.

"See ya tomorrow," I tell him as we reach the fence.

"Yep." He nods as he turns and starts goofing off down the street, kicking a pine cone flying like it's a soccer ball. He's not as bad as I thought he was, but I really don't understand the whole crush thing. He hardly knows me. Or maybe Lina invented the whole thing and it's another example of her version of fun.

My mouth feels a bit dry.

I remember I'm supposed to be hurrying so I swing my leg over the fence and hear, "Riley Jackson!"

The voice surprises me so much that I fall down the other side and straight into the bushes.

"Where have you been?"

I stand up, rubbing my arm where I hit the ground. Jess, the aftercare worker, is staring at me like I'm dead.

"Um . . ."

"Save it. Your mum's here. We were about to call the police."

I close my eyes. I wish I could disappear like I thought I could when I was four and playing hide-and-seek with my dad and Jenna. I try to swallow away the dryness in my mouth as I follow her through the garden and toward the aftercare office.

Mum must be standing near the window, watching, because she's suddenly outside the office, storming toward me with rage screaming all over her face. Then she stops in front of me and bends down so she's at my eye level.

I need to speak first. I go to say something but, instead of words, I vomit a stream of red and orange and brown all over her black leather heels. I could have at least saved the vomit stream for when I next saw Lina.

I'm sitting up in one of those hospital beds with stiff white sheets and machines beeping around me. Mum has barely spoken to me since she bought me here straight from school. She's sitting on the white chair in the corner, her eyes on her phone, and I'm leaning against the pillows, waiting for the emergency doctor to come and check me out so we can go home.

A woman about Mum's age pulls back the curtain. She's with the emergency nurse, who's a young guy with tattoos on both arms and spiky black hair. He's really funny and managed to avoid telling me off, which I'm sure I appreciated way more than Mum did.

"I'm Dr. Baldwin," says the woman.

Mum jumps to her feet and goes to shake the doctor's hand. "I'm Dr. Jackson," she says. Mum's a psychologist and I think it's a bit of a cheat to call herself a doctor, but she'd argue she's a doctor of the mind.

"This is Riley, a twelve-year-old with type one diabetes. She came in an hour ago, having vomited twice on the way here. Her mum's worried about diabetic ketoacidosis and her ketones were a little elevated at zero-point-six. We treated the high and need to do another blood sugar test," explains the nurse.

I hate being spoken about when I'm in the room. "I feel fine now."

The doctor steps closer to me and smiles briefly. I've been in emergency departments before but only twice for diabetes and that was when I was first diagnosed, and then when I had gastroenteritis and we couldn't get my blood sugar levels under control because I was vomiting so much.

"Nice to meet you, Riley," says the doctor, pushing her pale gray glasses up her nose.

"Can we go home? I'm sure I'm fine."

"What if it's DKA?" Mum says, stepping closer to me.

"It's not, Mum."

"How do you know?"

"Because I feel fine." I wish for once that Mum would listen to what I say about my body instead of always trying to take over.

I see the doctor share a quick look with the nurse. It's a look I'd give my dad if Mum was hounding me at home. The nurse turns and pats Mum on the arm. Inside I'm cheering because it's about as patronizing as Mum is with me sometimes. "Why don't we go and get a cup of coffee while Dr. Baldwin checks Riley out?"

Mum shakes her head. "No. I'm staying."

"Okay," says the nurse.

The doctor sits down on the edge of my bed. "So, what happened, Riley?"

"Um . . . I forgot to test," I say. But I don't tell her that I didn't test after lunchtime and I shared Tessa's cake and then had rice crackers and then a Slurpee. It's no wonder I had a high.

"She ran away from aftercare," snaps Mum.

The doctor keeps watching me, ignoring Mum. "Do you often forget to test?"

"Yes, she does. Her levels have been everywhere lately," says Mum.

"I need to hear from Riley." The doctor keeps her concentration on me.

I slump back on the bed. "I don't forget. It's just hard sometimes."

"Do you understand how serious it is? Your blood sugar levels were high. We do not want to be seeing ketones in your blood," she says.

I nod. This has been drilled into me since I was first diagnosed. I can almost hear Mum's lecture: *You could end up in a coma!* It's kind of true—when people who have diabetes don't get enough insulin, sugar builds up in their blood and it can't get out to give the body energy. When that happens, the body starts to break down fat for energy. That makes stuff called ketones, and when they build up they make you really sick—you start vomiting, you get really bad stomach pains, and yes, you can go into a coma. I knew the symptoms and the risks. I really didn't need to hear it again.

"Okay, well, I'm going to check you out and then I think we can probably send you home," she says. "We just need to do another test first."

Mum stares over the doctor's shoulder as the doctor checks my blood sugar levels and then does blood pressure tests. I watch Mum's face but all I can see is a grim line where her mouth is, like she's trying not to cry.

"It's not DKA. It's just a bad high that has started to correct itself," says the doctor. "I'm happy for you to go home but I do want you to make an appointment to see your endocrinologist next week. And I'll send her a letter explaining everything that happened. And make sure you test every two hours until your ketones are back to normal. Understood?"

I nod. "Yep."

"Appointment booked for Monday," says Mum.

I decide to keep my smart comment to myself and instead slide my feet into my dirty Converse so we can get out of here.

The adults make small talk while I lace my sneakers up, wishing that I didn't have to deal with any of this.

"Take care, Riley," says the doctor as I slowly follow Mum out of the cubicle and into the emergency ward.

"See ya," I say.

The ward is loud and busy. Babies scream behind curtains and kids chatter. Nurses hurry from one cubicle to the next, dragging gloves on and off their hands. I head through the glass doors after Mum.

She says nothing. Not walking to the car. Not when we are belted in. Not even when she starts driving. She says nothing and it's so much worse than if she spewed furious words at me.

"Mum?"

She shakes her head. "Not now."

"Mum," I try again, not able to wait.

"Riley, I'm so angry with you that if I talk I might say something

I'll regret. I will definitely talk to you about this, but not . . . now."

She stabs her finger at the radio and Mozart fills the car, and I feel like I'm running in circles on the netball court, yelling for the ball and being ignored by the rest of my team.

Chapter 17

MEG

IT'S FRIDAY, AND PEGGY IS coming to take Mum to see the doctor. That's about all I know. And that they spent three hours in the front room with the door shut a few days ago, until finally Peggy came out and squeezed me hard and told me I smelled like lasagna and fresh washing. I didn't tell her I hadn't bothered heating up the food, but that I'd just scoffed it cold from the container.

Peggy's eyes were red and ringed, but Mum looked even worse and went straight to bed. Peggy stayed for a bit, helping me do the dishes, and she told me stories about Dad. I'd heard most of them, but one of them made me laugh. It was when Dad tried to fry eggs on the hot concrete one summer because Peggy was hungry. I sort of listened and I sort of wondered about what had happened in the front room.

When she went to leave, I asked her. She smiled and tapped the end of my nose, her pink hair flatter than I'd ever seen.

"All you need to know is your mum is going to see a doctor and she's going to be okay."

I heard the words but didn't believe them. Not really. But when I left for school this morning, Mum was dressed. She told me Peggy was coming over and they were going to see someone. That's all she said. Then she wrapped me in a big hug and told me she loved me.

Riley isn't at school today, and I didn't go the past few days, so I still haven't seen her since she told Lina to leave me alone. We're supposed to present our graduation speeches to Mrs. Myer and do a practice run with Ms. Barber today. Instead of English this morning we are having a special "working bee," which means all of the grade six classrooms are full of graduation buzz. Banners are being decorated, menus written, and song lists argued about.

Ms. Barber has printed me out another copy of the form for the dinner. I'm supposed to invite my parents and my siblings. They have the chance to stand at the back of the gym and watch us eat dinner and make our speeches and then applaud us all as we listen to the band sing a farewell song. Then they have to leave so we can dance for a couple of hours with our friends. It sounds worse than a night of changing fuses and tinned tuna.

Right now, Lina and Tessa are huddled together with Nick and Matt in the corner, leaving Eleanora sitting alone at the large table with a huge sheet of white poster board and hundreds of colored pom-poms.

I know I risk being mocked or teased, but with only ten more days left of elementary school I figure I'm beyond injury. Besides, I suspect that Lina's distracted by Matt Park.

"Um . . . hi . . . ," I mumble.

Eleanora starts to smile, then looks up at me and her face freezes until it morphs into a look of horror. She flicks her eyes around to check the room, obviously wanting to know if Lina is watching.

"That pom-pom is actually pink, not blue, Eleanora," I tell her, pointing where a pink pom-pom disrupts the perfect sea of blue pom-poms.

"It's Elle. And what do you want, Meg?"

Eleanora doesn't look like she did when we fished on my couch for Dad's old socks. Or when we ate too much popcorn and she snorted orange juice from her nose. She doesn't look like she did when she fell from the monkey bars and broke her arm and I had to sit with her in the nurse's office wiping away the tears until the ambulance turned up.

She looks different. Her teeth are hiding behind purple braces just like Lina's. And her bangs are as straight as a ruler. But she still has trouble distinguishing some colors because she can't see the red element. She's color-blind. When we were friends, I thought it was the coolest thing in the world, because only about one in two hundred girls are.

"Where's Riley?" I ask her, aware that around us the rest of grade six are busily organizing and laughing and avoiding doing any real work because of graduation.

"She's sick," says Elle.

"Sick how?"

Elle shrugs and it reminds me of the day she walked past me in the playground at lunch and sat with Lina instead.

"Which one?" She looks back down at her pom-poms.

I point to the pink one, knowing I could actually point to a different one. But I once loved Eleanora so much I thought we were kindred spirits. She plucks the pink pom-pom off the desk and looks for a blue one. I know she's having trouble distinguishing the color, so I grab it and hold it out to her. It's soft and light and as bright as Peggy's hair was before she went pink.

"Sorry about the other day," she says in the smallest of whispers, as if she's afraid of uttering the words.

Surprised by the apology, I hand her the pom-pom and leave her to it. As I sit down at a table for one and open my half-written speech, I can't stop thinking about what would have happened if Eleanora and I had stayed friends. There was no reason why we stopped hanging out. We didn't fight. We didn't even disagree. It was just that Lina decided to add Eleanora to her group. And I guess Lina had more appeal than me. It was about the time my dad died and I was probably not much fun anymore. I had bundles of sadness weighing me down and I wasn't sure how to balance what I felt on the inside with who I was supposed to be on the outside.

"Can't wait to see what you've written, Meg," says Ms. Barber, dragging a white plastic chair over to sit close.

"I've made a start," I tell her as she slides the page toward her.

I watch as Ms. Barber reads the five or so lines I've written and rewritten so many times I could speak them without any prompting.

She finishes and sits back on her chair, looking at me until I have to look away. "I think you could come up with more . . . truth."

"I know it's not great, but it's what we were told to write."

"Meg, your essays and stories are beautiful. You craft words really well. This is . . . and please don't be offended . . . it's dull."

I lay my arms across the speech, not wanting the words to be seen. "I told you I didn't want to write one."

"Yes, but you don't always get to decide what you do and do not want to do."

I sigh, wondering if she knows how true that is. "Fine. I'll go to the nurse's office and finish it there." I stand up and start to grab my things.

"No. You can't just go to the nurse's office. I've been far too lenient about that this year."

"But . . ."

She shakes her head. "Sorry, Meg."

I sink back down into the chair, dreading having to stay here until lunch. She's never said no to me before. Is this what junior high will be? Teachers who make me stay?

"Write your speech. I know you can."

I let her leave the table and I drop my head down, wishing I'd stayed home again after all. But I missed Riley yesterday and I was really hoping to see her today.

Behind me Lina laughs and walks past with Tessa. Lina pauses as she reaches my table.

"This isn't taken, is it?"

"No."

"Great. We can chat while we work," she says, sitting down in the seat that Ms. Barber just left.

I roll my eyes at her, wondering what she's about to deliver and doubting she can do too much damage when a teacher is around.

"What's your speech about, Meg?"

"School."

"Sounds fascinating," she says, causing someone on the other side of her to giggle.

I look around for Ms. Barber and see her watching from the other side of the room. I make sure she can see my face distort as I try to drag breath noisily into my chest. I cough, although it sounds like the air is stuck in my throat. I make a choking sound and drop my head down onto the table.

"Meg? You okay?"

I can hear the words but I can't look up. I feel someone rubbing my back in circles like Mum when I was little and I couldn't sleep.

"Meg . . . let's go outside. . . . Come on. . . ."

Hands slide under my arms, lifting me up, carrying me out. I hear Lina laugh. Someone else, too. But at least I'm out of their range here. I'm helped to sit down on a cold metal step near the door. The cold seeps into my legs through my jeans. Ms. Barber sits beside me, her hand still rubbing my back.

"Breathe in and hold it. . . . One, two, three . . . and out."

I can hear her shushing me, whispering to me over and over that it will be okay, if I just breathe.

I breathe. And look up behind me into the window at the front of the common space. I see Lina's face pressed against the glass. Usually I avoid Lina, but maybe avoidance isn't the best strategy after all. Maybe I need to fight her head-on. Using my hand as a blinker so Ms. Barber can't see, I stare up at Lina, meeting her gaze, wondering what Anne with an *e* would do.

"It's okay. Just a panic attack," says Ms. Barber. "I've had a few of these in my time too. You'll be okay."

I nod and start to slow my breathing. I wonder if this relief is what Riley feels at the end of a low. "It's just Lina. She's making things hard."

"I'll talk to her."

"Thank you. If you could."

"You feel up to coming back in?"

I shake my head. "No."

"Okay, then. Straight to the nurse's office, just until you feel better," she says quietly. "In junior high, you won't have Lina around to annoy you, thank goodness," she adds, and I wonder if she's just broken some sort of schoolteacher conduct, and then decide that I like her even more than I did this morning.

Chapter 18

RILEY

IT'S BEEN FIVE DAYS SINCE I visited emergency and it's like I'm under house arrest. Mum wouldn't let me go to school until I saw Eda, who was also pretty unimpressed by my recent behavior. She actually lectured me about the dangers of eating and not testing and sided with the Brain about my friendship group.

I felt like saying, *What friendship group?* I don't think I have one anymore. And even if I do, I'm not sure I want to. I messaged them to say I was sick and the only one who responded was Elle, but even she stopped texting after the first day. The whole "Slurpee incident," as Jenna's calling it, made me realize that Lina doesn't care about me. And if I'm ever going to have a chance at convincing Mum I can be responsible, then I need to look after myself properly. Which means testing at school and not drinking Slurpees without putting in grams first.

Mum hasn't really been talking to me since the Slurpee incident. It feels like the thick, humid Sydney air before a summer storm, when the pressure builds and you know what's coming but there's nothing you can do to avoid the downpour.

She places a plate of carrot sticks, rice crackers, and hummus down in front of me. "Put in fifteen," she says. "But do a test first, please."

Instead of eating the carrot sticks, I arrange them as upright poles, using the hummus as cement. It's an impressive-looking vegetable sculpture by the time I finish.

"Don't play with your food, Riley," Mum says, wandering into the dining room and placing a vase of roses from the garden in the middle of the table.

"I'm not hungry."

Only my mum can make sighing into a conversational skill. I know exactly what she's thinking. She pulls out the chair next to me and I groan.

"Mum, I know you think this is all on me, but you made me leave Lina's party early and now I have no friends."

She scoffs and I wish the carrots were spears so I could stab them into her skin.

"I let you go to the party . . . and of course you have friends."

"You know what I mean, Mum. You make me different. Every day. I'm different. You tell me that diabetes shouldn't hold me back, but you make me stand out from everyone else!"

My heart is racing like I'm having a high, but I'm not high, I'm just angry. It feels good to understand my body, to know that the itch under my skin and tightness across my neck is from emotion, and not because of blood sugar levels.

"You are different," she says quietly. "You have diabetes. It's not a part-time condition. It's serious, Riley."

I pick up the plate and slam it down on the table, hard enough to knock over all the carrot sticks. I wish I'd done it hard to enough to smash the plate.

"I know that! It's my body."

"And you're my child. I have to look after your body until you're old enough to look after it yourself."

Mum never raises her voice. She uses this clipped, firm tone like I'm a patient of hers, like I'm someone who is paying her to tell me what's wrong. And I hate it.

"I'll never be old enough, Mum. You control everything I do. All the time! You don't control Jenna. She's out doing whatever she wants."

I see her look of interest and I know I've gone too far.

"What do you mean, Jenna's 'out doing whatever she wants'?"

I shake my head. "Nothing. I didn't mean anything."

"You sure, Riley?"

"Yep."

She reaches for my arm and I pull away so quickly that I almost whack her by mistake.

Dad comes into the dining room and hovers in the doorway like he's not sure if he wants in or out. Usually he'd still be at work now, but for some reason he's here, like I need double monitoring. He rarely gets involved in the diabetes stuff so I'm not expecting he's about to start now. But he walks over to where Mum is sitting, rests his hand on the top of her back, and starts rubbing her shoulders.

"I think we need to talk about why you left aftercare," he says quietly.

"I said sorry!"

He shakes his head. "That's not enough, Riley."

"Dad, it wasn't my fault."

Mum laughs and the sound is cold and hard. "Lina made you leave? She's that powerful?"

"No. It just happened. I was trying to make it up to her that I'd left her party early." But it sounds so stupid when I say it.

"I know you think we're trying to stop you from living, but we're not," says Dad.

"No, we're just trying to give you a life," says Mum.

"What does that even mean?" I spit the words at them both.

Mum starts nodding her head strangely and Dad reaches over for her hand, and I realize that she's crying and I really don't want to see that because she never cries.

"Riley . . . when you were diagnosed, you'd been sick for weeks. Months . . . ," says Dad.

"Yeah, I remember."

"And I didn't take you to the doctor. I didn't take it seriously," adds Mum.

"So? What's that got to do with anything?"

"You could have died!" she shouts, banging her hand so

hard on the table that the carrots topple into the hummus. "Do you understand?"

Now she looks up at me and I see the lines in her face and the softness that's sometimes there and I don't know what to say.

"Riley? Do you understand what I'm saying?"

"I think so. You feel guilty and so you won't let me do anything," I tell her.

Dad leaps on my words like I've tossed a grenade and cowered behind a wall to watch it explode. "Riley, that's enough."

But Mum starts to laugh, and it's not cold or hard or anything. It's just a laugh. "That's probably about right. Pretty accurate, really. Maybe you can come into the family business when you leave school. You might make a fine head doctor," she says, watching me.

"Really? You feel guilty?"

She shrugs and her shoulders start to shake and Dad wraps himself around her as if to protect her from unraveling any further, and I wish Jenna would come home from "choir" or wherever she actually is and save me.

"Don't, Mum. It's not your fault what happened. It's not your fault I have diabetes. It just is."

She's shaking her head and nodding her head and I have no idea if she's agreeing with me or not, but at least we're talking about things in a different way.

"I know I shouldn't have skipped out of aftercare and I won't ever do that again. I know I shouldn't have drunk a

Slurpee without testing and I won't do that again, either. But I do want to go to parties and go shopping with friends and learn to do a line change. I'm going to be thirteen soon . . ."

"In seven months!"

"Yep, Mum, that's soon. And I want some freedom. Okay?"

"Let's just take it slowly, Riley, okay?"

"Mum, I've been taking it slowly for twelve years and five months. Any slower and I'll be a hundred before my first sleepover."

Mum smiles and it reaches all the way to her eyes. "You probably won't be wanting sleepovers when you're one hundred," she jokes.

One. Two. Three . . .

"Are you counting before you speak?"

I nod. "Yeah. Five!"

"You know that I'm overprotective because I love you. But I'm coming to understand that it's not what you need anymore."

"And?"

"And . . . I'll teach you to manage your diabetes yourself," she says, reaching for my hand.

"Really? All of it?"

She holds up her fingers measuring a tiny amount, maybe less than a centimeter. And I laugh. It's a start.

Chapter 19

MEG

MY HAND SHAKES ONLY A little when I put the key in the front door. I'm not sure what to expect. Will Mum be in bed? Will the curtains be closed? Will the house smell musty, like the air is trapped and sad?

I head inside, pausing. Something's different. The air smells spicy. I walk farther down the hall.

"Meg? Is that you? I'm in here."

I stop at the door to the kitchen. Mum's at the stove with a wooden spoon in her hand. She's stirring a pot.

"Mum?"

I step across the threshold, onto the black-and-white tiles. The benches are clean and wiped down. Something is bubbling in the frying pan. There are chunks of meat and potatoes and a rich brown sauce. "What is it?"

"Not sure . . ."

I smile. "What's it supposed to be?"

"Stew."

"It looks stew . . . ish . . ." I take the wooden spoon from her hand and dipping it in for a taste test. "Mmm. Better than tins of tuna," I say.

"I thought you liked tins of tuna," says Mum.

I shake my head. "No. I hate tuna."

"Me too."

I hand back the spoon, wondering how I can ask about her day without setting something off.

"Peggy and I ate an entire Boston bun today," says Mum, stirring the meat around.

"Yum."

"And she dropped this off!"

"Oh . . . I thought you cooked it," I say.

Mum shakes her head. "I think I've forgotten how to cook. But I can reheat."

She flicks the switch on the stove, turning off the gas. "So, I have a doctor now. Her name's Margaret," she says.

"Another Margaret?"

"I took it as a good sign. But this one calls herself her full name. I liked her. We talked for two hours."

"Okay."

"And she told me what was wrong with me."

I fidget with my hands. I don't know where to put them and I can't be still.

"She thinks that losing your dad made me depressed and the panic attacks are all part of it. But she thinks she can help."

I reach into my pocket and touch the corner of the Bag.

Mum shuffles closer. "And so can Peggy. She's going to lend us some money until I can go back to work. We can buy you shoes and your school uniform. No more tuna. I should have let her help before."

She reaches me, her hands snaking around until they take mine. Then I make myself look at her. Really look at her. And I see that she's crying. Streams of tears silently make their way down over her cheekbones and drip off the edges like a waterfall.

If she's crying, I will. And I don't want to. Not yet. Not here.

I pull free. "I've got homework, Mum."

She tries to hold on to me, but I'm moving out of reach.

"Meg . . ."

"Mum . . ." I don't know what to do with this.

"Meg . . ."

She circles me this time and I can't back out. I feel her head burrowing into my neck, her tears wet on my skin.

"I'm sorry," she says. "I've been missing so much. I just hurt. I loved your dad and . . . and . . ."

There's an avalanche—no, a tidal wave—no, a volcano of feeling flowing inside my head. The pressure is building. The eruption is going to take out our entire street.

We don't do apologies.

"I'm really sorry . . . about how . . . how missing I've been since your dad died. . . ."

When this starts, I won't be able to stop the flow. I should leave before I blow up right in front of her, but she's wrapped me so tight that when it comes she smothers the full brunt of it into her chest. There's a boom.

And I sob and sob and sob.

It's late and the house is quiet. I should be asleep but I'm having trouble tonight. It's the Bag's fault. It's keeping me awake. I head down the hallway to Mum's room.

I shuffle around at the door, my feet marking the carpet in tracks. I'm not sure if I should go in or not.

Mum's room is dark, but I can hear her breathing.

"Mum?" I whisper, squeezing the Bag tight in my hand and moving forward. Now that I'm here I can't turn back.

She snuffles as I edge closer to the bed, though I think she's asleep. I walk around to Dad's side and a slice of cool air blows over me from the open window. I slide into the crisp sheets and lie down, the Bag getting in the way. I reach back toward Dad's side table, open his drawer, place the Bag inside, and close it quietly. Then I roll back toward Mum, slide my arm around her warm body, and curl up close.

Chapter 20

RILEY

IT'S TUESDAY AND I'M FINALLY back at school. After a visit to the principal's office, I'm now heading down the corridor to the nurse's office.

Dash is sitting in the corner chair when I come in. He's reading a graphic novel and grinning to himself.

"Hey, Dash." I sit down on the edge of the bed and wait for him to look up.

"Hey."

"Good book?"

He raises an eyebrow like he's amused at my lack of conversational ability.

"She's not here," he says, closing the book but keeping his hand inside to mark his place, as if he's only prepared to give me a second of his time.

"I can see that."

"No offense, but I'm really glad you guys will be gone soon. All this will be mine!" He looks around and smiles like it's all one big joke. "I'll just need to find some friends to hang out in here with me."

"You've got heaps of friends, haven't you?"

"None that understand the power of the nurse's office."

I smile. He's right. This place is something else.

"If you see her . . . ," I tell him, standing up.

"Don't you already have enough friends?"

"I'm not really hanging out with your sister anymore," I tell him, realizing how strange it is that I haven't given much thought to Lina and the others. I just want to find Meg.

"Good for you."

"Okay, see ya."

"Hey, Riley, those quotes Meg's always saying? In case you were wondering, they're from *Anne of Green Gables*."

"Thanks."

I head back to the grade six classroom building, bored already by the endless graduation chatter. It's on Thursday night this week and it's all anyone is talking about. Meg's right. It's stupid. As if anyone doesn't graduate from primary school.

"Hey . . . feel like jacking a car later?"

I spin around. "Meg!"

She's standing on the landing near the grade six common space, reading a book. I walk over and immediately notice her feet. Her slippers have gone. She's wearing brand-new blue sneakers.

"Mum bought me new shoes," she says, noticing me staring.

"Nice."

"I don't know. I miss my slippers," she says.

"Yeah, I bet they were pretty comfortable."

"I had to give Ms. Barber my speech," she says, holding up a sheet of paper.

"Mrs. Myer just read mine this morning because I was away last week. Made notes in red. To be honest, I had to change a sentence and make it about positive experiences because she thought it was a bit negative."

Meg smiles and it's mysterious and playful. "She won't like mine, then!"

"Can I have a read?"

She shakes her head. "Nope."

The bell rings and I see Meg become aware of where she is. She clocks the others moving toward us like a giant wave. I wait for her to scurry, to run, to flee to the nurse's office where she's safe and protected.

But she doesn't.

She steps closer.

We're like a little island in the middle of a tsunami.

"New shoes, Slipper Girl," I hear someone say.

Meg's eyes find mine. Her jaw looks set. Her shoulders drop. She's ready.

"Why you talking to *her*, R?" says Lina, strolling to where we stand.

"Her name's Meg," I say, staring straight at Lina. Elle and

Tessa are tucked in behind her. The three of them are all in their usual uniform of denim jackets and tiny shorts.

"Didn't realize you two were such good friends," says Lina.

There's a crowd gathering around us now. Meg and I are in the middle. Lina, too. It's like all of grade six is hovering to see what will happen next. I'm really hoping that Meg's body doesn't decide it would be a good time for a panic attack.

"Yeah . . . well, we are . . . ," I say.

Lina steps up into my space. I swallow hard. This is not what I wanted.

"I thought we were friends," Lina says just to me.

"We are. I mean, we were." I feel a tug of something in my chest. "Not anymore," I tell her, my heart speeding up like it does when I'm having a high.

She shakes her head, her mouth mean and hard. "Did she tell you she got me in trouble the other day?"

Curious, I look at Meg, who whispers, "It's a pleasure, Lina. Anytime."

"Obviously, R, you can't have normal friends. Only sick friends," says Lina.

She points at Meg and Meg shuffles around, looking down at the ground. This must be making her pretty uncomfortable. Having an audience is not really her thing.

"You okay, Meg?"

Next to me Meg starts coughing and clutches at her throat.

"Leave her alone, Lina. The bell just rang. Let's just get to class," I say, trying to move away. But she isn't done with us. With me.

I shoot a look at Meg. Her breathing is raspy and raw beside me.

"Can't believe you chose her, R," she says. "Of all the people." Then she turns dramatically and storms off, her minions scurrying after her.

"Why not? She's funny, smart, and loyal!" I yell after her. I turn to Meg.

"You okay?"

She straightens up and her breathing changes. "Yep. All good."

I take in the size of her smile and her clear eyes. Then I notice how straight she's standing and how relaxed her face looks. "But the panic attack?"

"It's fine. I'm okay now."

"Wait, were you faking?"

"Today I was."

I clench my jaw. "What about the other day on the track?"

"That one was real. Sometimes I have them, and sometimes I pretend to have them. Panic attacks mean that Sarah feeds me. That Ms. Barber doesn't call on me to speak up in class. And it means I get to go to the nurse's office whenever I need."

"But you don't have to go. I do! I have no choice, and you're faking panic attacks so you can too." My voice is too loud and I'm aware that kids are watching us as they hurry past to their classes. But I don't care. Right now, I'm the ticking bomb.

"I have them sometimes."

"But, I . . . I . . ."

"Felt sorry for me?"

"No. Yeah . . . I don't know. You lied."

Meg closes her eyes and pushes her fringe out of her face. "I didn't lie all the time. And when I did, it was because I needed to, so that doesn't count."

"You hang in the nurse's office but you aren't properly sick. Just sometimes you can't breathe properly."

She shrugs at me like I've got it all wrong but my skin is itching and I scratch at my neck and I feel angry. "You're normal, Meg!"

Her face is shocked. I just yelled at her and now I feel bad, but I also feel furious.

"Normal? Why? Because I don't have diabetes? Because I'm not an asthmatic? Because I don't always need to breathe into a bag? Nobody's normal, Riley. We're all just trying to cope."

She leans down, picks up her schoolbag, then turns and faces me. "That's the worst of growing up, and I'm beginning to realize it. The things you wanted so much when you were a child don't seem half so wonderful to you when you get them."

"Don't quote Anne-of-something at me!" I yell.

Her eyes widen. "It's not 'Anne-of-something.' It's *Anne of Green Gables*. Here, you should read it sometime."

And she slides the old book she was reading into my hands and walks past me without looking back.

Chapter 21

MEG

MY HEAD IS BENT OVER the industrial-sized sink. Peggy's fingers are working their way through my hair, washing out all the gunk.

"You sure you checked with your mum?"

"Yes, though she was asleep when I asked her."

Peggy laughs and it makes her fingers wiggle against my scalp.

"How's she doing?"

I smile into the metal, loving that Peggy always checks in. "She likes Margaret. Though it's going to take a while for her to be normal again," I say, wondering why I chose the word that Riley tossed at me earlier today. I decide I need to clarify. "I mean back to who she was, not like everyone else. I don't actually think there is a normal."

"No. I don't, either."

She drapes a towel across my head and tightens it around the back of my neck. "You dry. I'll go and make tea."

I towel my hair roughly, desperate to see what it looks like. There's a little mirror in the back room, but I decide not to check until it's dry.

I plug in the hair dryer and stand with my head upside down above the sink, fluffing my hair with the warm air. I think about Riley and how upset she was today, how much I hurt her without intending to. And I wonder how she knew where my quotes came from.

Last night I burned all of the Bags in the metal fire pit in the backyard. It didn't take long. About three seconds for the *whoosh* of flame and then they were all turned to ash. Except for one; I left the mushroom bag in Dad's drawer, mainly because it was the only one I'd introduced to Riley. And also because I might actually need it again. Mum wants me to see my own version of Margaret, to talk about everything that's happened and also how sometimes I can't breathe properly when things are hard. I didn't know she knew about that. But she does. I agreed to go and talk to a doctor, because it doesn't seem right that she has to go and I can avoid it.

My fingers snake through a pile of knots and catch in the mess. I turn off the hair dryer, hoping my hair's dry enough so that I can see the effect.

Peggy squeals as I skip through into the back room. "Whoa!"

"Good whoa?"

She nods and grins, gives me a thumbs-up, and hands me

a mirror. I look into it and cannot believe the face staring back at me.

"Oh!" My hair is a bright carrot-orange red and, strangely, I look more like me than I used to. I move the mirror from one side to the other, trying to see all of it.

Peggy is behind me, clutching at my shoulders. "Do you like it?"

I nod. "Yes. I think I do. Now I look like Anne. Anne with an *e*."

"You do. It's the reddest of reds, Miss Anne," says Peggy. "I do believe that red hair shall be your joy."

I spin around and hug her. "That's not the quote, Peggy, although I love it. Thank you!"

"Good. I hope your mum does too. I'm a bit scared she'll be angry with me!"

"If she is, then we'll know she's getting better, because she hasn't cared enough about anything to be angry for a very long time."

Peggy spins me around in a silly circle. "I think I might have to go red next! I've been far too boring having pink hair for weeks. Now, shall we have cake?"

"I'd like that very much."

My red hair leaves a stain on the white pillowcase that I'm sure Peggy will know how to get out.

Mum wasn't exactly angry about Peggy dying my hair,

but she wasn't very impressed, either. I tried to explain that I wanted to look like Anne Shirley, but she thought I should be happy looking like me.

But I feel like I've changed from the old me, and red hair is a sign of that. Normally I'm up before Mum, but this morning I can hear her puttering around in the kitchen. She's seeing Margaret again today. She's going twice a week, at the moment, and that means she has to leave the house. She didn't want to go by herself, so Peggy has said she can take her to the appointments for as long as she needs.

I don't want to go to school today. They'll be decorating the gym all day and everyone will be jittery and giggly and I'm not sure how Riley will react if she sees me. I can't stop thinking about her, and how different things are since I met her. Though each time she creeps into my head, I force her out again.

"You getting up, honey?" Mum's standing in the door, sipping from a mug with a badly drawn, faded face on it that I haven't seen her use in ages. It was the mug Dad always drank from, one I made him for Father's Day in kindergarten, but when she stopped working, she hid it away in the cupboard.

"I thought maybe I'd stay home. I'm not sure I can cope with today," I tell her as honestly as I can. We've talked about trying to be more open with each other. It's hard because for a long time I've pretended with Mum as much as I have with anyone.

She steps into my room, and I think it might be the first time for a while. "I'm sure you can."

"I'm not sure I want to, then."

She nods. "Isn't it graduation tonight? Sarah phoned to make sure we were attending. She said if it was a financial issue, the school could cover it."

"Oh."

"Do you want to go?"

I see a flash of red hair as I shake my head.

"Why not? She said you'd written a speech."

I can't believe Sarah phoned Mum. I had no idea she did things like that. I wonder what else she's been ringing her about. Although that would explain how Mum knew I had panic attacks.

"Ms. Barber is going to deliver it."

"Maybe you should go."

"No. I don't think so."

She nods like she gets it and I'm amazed that she does. Parents in books always push their children into things they don't want to do, and I'm so relieved she isn't doing that.

"I know taking advice from a mother who has barely been out of the house in the past year might seem strange, but if your speech is half as good as I'm sure it is, then I would've thought you'd want to deliver it yourself."

I roll my eyes at her and lift the pillow over my head, not caring that I'm about to stain the other side of the pillowcase too.

"Is there another reason you don't want to go to school?"

Mum asks. She sits down on the edge of my bed and tugs at the pillow, trying to lift it from me. I let her move it down a bit, but keep my eyes scrunched closed. I'm still not really used to her wanting to be so close.

"Come on, Meg. You can tell me."

I roll over and see Mum's concerned face. She hasn't looked at me like that for a long time.

"I lied to my friend," I tell Mum finally.

"Did you have a good reason?"

I nod.

"Then just explain it," she says quietly, her fingers working their way through my red hair.

"Really?"

"Really."

Without the Bag to keep me company, I have nothing for my hands to play with. I don't have my book, either, because I gave it to Riley. I'm practicing one of Mum's breathing techniques that her doctor showed her. She says they help. In the end, I wait in my corner chair and listen to the humming fridge.

Mum and I ate breakfast together this morning. Outside in the garden, where she said my hair shone like a beacon in the sunlight. We talked about Dad. Not much, but a bit. And she cooked eggs. They were rubbery but they filled me up.

I hear Dash's voice in the hall outside the nurse's office.

The door pushes open. Dash grins at me.

"Meg, meet Riley. . . . Riley, meet Meg. . . ."

Riley bangs into him and sees me in the chair. Her face changes and I realize Dash hasn't told her I was waiting.

"Hi . . . ," I whisper. Dash shrugs at me like he's tried his best and then slips out past Riley and disappears down the corridor.

From the doorway, Riley stares at me. "You have red hair!"

"I do."

"Just like Anne Shirley."

"How do you know Anne Shirley?"

She steps forward, letting the door to the nurse's office close behind her. "I started reading your book. It's pretty good. Except she's too dramatic sometimes."

I swallow hard. I really don't know what to say.

"What? No quotes?" she says, moving over to the bed and perching on the edge.

"I could never express all my sorrow, no, not if I used up a whole dictionary," I tell her.

"See, dramatic!"

"Okay, I'm sorry for lying. I'm sorry I made stuff up and I'm sorry I hurt you," I say, looking down at the ground.

"Mum said I had to forgive you. She said she liked you when she met you. Much more than she ever liked Lina. And she knew all about *Anne of Green Gables*," says Riley. Then she looks up at me. "And I get why you wanted to escape sometimes. We were mean to you. I guess you felt you had no choice."

My chest rises like I don't have enough air, but it's not a panicked feeling, just a hopeful one. "Does that mean we're . . . friends?"

Riley looks up at me. Then she unzips her fanny pack and pulls out her jelly beans. She holds out the bag to me and I take one.

"Friends? Yeah. I guess it does, Meg with a *g*," she says as she tosses an orange jelly bean up into the air and I catch it in my hand.

Chapter 22

RILEY

WHEN I GET HOME FROM school that afternoon, Mum hands me a large white shopping bag, which is pretty surprising because she always refuses bags when we buy anything. And this one is thick and glossy and definitely not something we can add to the compost. I slide my hands in and pull out something wrapped in white tissue paper with a gold embossed sticker holding the lot together.

I rip the package open and spy the perfect blue dress I tried on so many weeks ago. "Really? You bought it?"

"I did."

"Thanks, Mum!" I jump up and crush her in an awkward hug.

"It's practical. I like the pocket," she says, hugging me back.

"And it looks nice," says Jenna. "That's what you're supposed to say, Mum!"

"Yes, it does," Mum adds.

I smile at her and then at my sister. "I'm not sure how long I'll last tonight. I might just eat my burger and come home with you guys."

"It's graduation!" Jenna says, outraged that I wouldn't want to make the most of it.

"You can go to the dance for an hour. Ms. Barber's going to be there. I've already spoken to her," says Mum.

"You spoke to my teacher?"

Mum nods. "Yes. I had to make sure a responsible adult would be on duty."

I try not to groan. "But . . . Mum . . ."

"If you're going to say you're responsible, don't. I told you this would take time, Riley."

Jenna holds up her hands. "Can we talk about this later? It's going to take ages for me to fix Riley's hair!"

I nod, which encourages Jenna to grab my arm and drag me up the stairs.

As Dad pulls up outside school, I see a limo stretched long and silver in front of the school gates and watch as Lina, Tessa, and Elle climb out from the back seat in their matching navy dresses with sparkly gold shoes. Jenna reaches across and squeezes my hand. She's guessed something's up.

"A limo! What are those parents thinking?" Mum says, until Dad whispers something and causes her to stop. Usually Mum being all judgy would frustrate me but tonight I'm sort of relieved. If the only way I can survive the next few hours is to listen to Mum be outraged and shocked by Lina, then that's what I'll have to do.

"Come on, kiddo. Let's go grab a good spot for photos," says Dad.

There are groups meeting on the track, posing with their friends for teary parents to snap off some memories. I get to stand with my sister and then with my mum so Dad can do the same. Then Jenna tells us all to crowd in and she holds her arm out as far as she can and clicks a crooked selfie.

The air feels electric around us. Like we've waited seven years for this. And suddenly the idea of graduating doesn't feel so stupid. It's a chance to celebrate a place we've all spent time in together before we move on to the next thing. I just wish I was celebrating with friends too, but the one person I want to be here with said she wasn't coming.

"You ready, Riley?" Mum says, smoothing my dress across my shoulders.

"Not really."

"You'll be fine. Come on."

She holds out her elbow so that I can hook my arm into the crook and we walk along the tatty red carpet that's stained and dirty from the feet of hundreds of grade six kids who have graduated before us. My diabetes kit is tucked into the pocket of the dress and the material doesn't pull across my stomach. I'm wearing lip gloss but not too much, and I look just like everyone else.

Inside, most of the kids are already seated at their tables. Mum smiles at me, unhooks her arm, and follows Dad and Jenna down the back to where all the onlookers stand. My legs feel a bit shaky and my feet rub in Jenna's old black shoes that don't quite fit. But I'm trying to pretend that I belong.

I see Lina, Elle, and Tessa sitting at one end of a long table with an empty chair on the right. That's mine. I guess nobody thought to move me at the last minute.

"Hi," I say, sitting down.

"You wore blue," says Lina, and for once I can't read her tone.

So I nod and hope we can just eat and not talk and I can say my speech and leave.

"No Slipper Girl, then?" says Lina.

"Lina, you seem to have a lot of trouble remembering her name. It's Meg. And no, she's not coming, but I really wish she was."

Lina and Tessa and Elle move their chairs closer together and I can hear them giggling and whispering. It looks like it's going to be a long night with the three of them playing whatever game they are still playing.

The burgers are carried on trays and delivered to students by helping parents and teachers. Ms. Barber smiles as she slides a burger down in front of me.

"Your mum said you'd know how many grams, but if you don't then I can tell you," she says, whispering it as close as she can so that the others can't hear.

And I laugh at Mum, even though she can't see me. "Thanks."

I don't feel like eating a burger. Not sitting here with Lina and the others, waiting to speak in front of all these people, but I put in some grams for half the burger and force myself to take a few bites. Everyone else is eating and talking and laughing, and I glance around the gym at the balloons and the banners and Elle's pom-poms, which don't seem to be stuck properly onto the wall because there are pom-poms lying on the floor.

Onstage, photos flash across a big screen. It's of all of us as babies and kids. People call out as they spy familiar faces but I just watch as one image morphs into the next. Red cheeks, brown hair, pink lips, light skin, dark skin, glasses, freckles. It's all there.

Suddenly the stage lights brighten. Mrs. Myer clips onto the stage in her heels and yet another brown dress and starts speaking into the microphone, which isn't turned on so nobody can hear her. She tries again and this time the sound distorts and muffles until it's fixed. Finally, she starts her speech to the room of graduating students, banging on and on about elementary school and what it means to be transitioning to junior high. I tune out, knowing I'm on soon.

And just at that minute I look across to the gym door and see Meg.

Chapter 23

MEG

MUM FALTERS AS WE STEP through the doors onto the polished wooden floor. I feel her body tense and hear Peggy whispering to her on the other side. Together, we move her into the gym, where Mrs. Myer is addressing the crowd.

"Mum? You okay?" I say quietly.

She nods but focuses on her feet, like it's all she can do to keep walking. I know how hard this is for her. We reach the back corner and position her as far away from the other parents as we can, against the wall with Peggy beside her.

"Can our speakers for the night please make their way to the stage," says Mrs. Myer.

"Wish me luck," I say to them both.

Mum manages to squeeze my hand and look at me. She smiles as her eyes focus on mine. I see her straighten her shoulders and nod. I know she's going to be okay. Maybe not always, and maybe not right away, but soon.

She leans across and whispers in my ear, "You're my girl."

It was something Dad used to say, and it makes me take a deep breath. Although the idea that he's sort of here is special, too. Peggy must see I'm wobbly, because she tousles my hair and then tells me that I'll be wonderful and she'll film the lot and use it to embarrass me at my twenty-first birthday.

I start the long walk past the tables toward the front of the gym. Cameras are flashing everywhere and parents line the back of the gym, ten deep.

"You came!" Riley darts in front of me. She's in a blue dress and her long hair is pinned up, and she's even taller than usual.

"You look amazing!"

She grabs both of my hands. "I'm so happy you're here."

"Me too."

She grins at me and I grin back, and we're frozen in a smile-fest.

Mrs. Myer finishes her speech and I hear her introduce Tom. That means we're on in a minute and we're still down here near the tables.

"Come on!" I tell Riley.

"I like your slippers," she whispers as we hurry toward the stage.

"Thanks."

"I'm so glad to see you, Meg," Ms. Barber whispers to me as

we step up onto the side of the stage. Like me, she's not wearing a dress. She's in the same jeans she wears every day, but her hair is spiky and standing to attention. She looks great.

I see Dash waving madly from the PA system. He's in charge of making sure the microphones are loud enough. I'm glad he's here. He looks different outside the nurse's office. Perhaps we all do.

Tom's speech is boring and predictable but it's met with a wild round of applause. Matteo's speech is a bit funnier but the content doesn't change too much. I look out into the audience. The lights are so bright up here that I can't see the faces, not even Lina. It's just a blur of noise and color.

Riley is introduced next and I watch as she walks up to the microphone. She looks dreamy, like she's just stepped out of a painting. She pulls a small sheet of paper from her dress pocket, clears her throat, and starts to read.

"Hi, I'm Riley Jackson. Tonight I'm here to talk about what this school has meant to me. I got chosen to make a speech tonight because I'm different. I'm diabetic. Nobody actually said that was why I got chosen, but we all know it. The thing is, I don't want to talk about being diabetic. It's really boring. But it's what makes me different. Just like Ms. Barber has lots of ear piercings, and Nick Zarro has freckles, I have diabetes.

"To be honest, diabetes doesn't stop me from being who I am, but it does mean I have to do things differently sometimes. I've always hated that. Now I'm working out that it's not so bad.

And that's really thanks to meeting Meg Tower in the nurse's office.

"Most of you probably visited the nurse's office once or twice in your time here. But for some of us"—Riley looks across at Dash and then catches my eye—"it's been a second home. A tiny, horrible, bright room with vinyl-covered furniture and an old poster on the wall, it's become somewhere special. It was where I learned who I really am. Normal. Not normal. Just like all of you. And it was where I got to understand what friendship really means, and how to be me: Riley Jackson. Thank you."

Everyone starts cheering as Riley walks off the stage. When she gets to me, she smiles, the spotlight overhead illuminating her face. She just made a speech about the nurse's office and she totally nailed it.

It's my turn next.

When Mrs. Myer calls my name, there is a smattering of laughter from the gym. Though tonight I don't care at all. I walk onstage. The microphone is set too high and I fumble with it, trying to move it down, but instead I make it fall, causing static screeching to fill the hall. Then I realize I don't have my speech. Ms. Barber sees me drowning and realizes what's happened. She dashes onto the stage to hand me the piece of paper I gave her the other day.

"Like the red hair, by the way!" she whispers.

"Thanks."

I wait until she's scampered off before I lean forward and

start talking. "I'm Margaret. Meg. Slipper Girl, Nurse's Office Girl. I go by many names. . . ."

I look out into the lights, trying to face them.

"Most of you don't know me at all. We've been at school together for seven years and you don't know the first thing about me. You think I wear slippers because I'm poor or because I'm weird. Well tonight, I wear slippers because they're much more comfortable than high heels."

A few people laugh, though this time I think it's nice laughter, like they get it. I take a big breath and force my words out louder.

"Elementary school has not been the best years of my life. Sorry if that's a shock, Mrs. Myer. Actually, it's often been pretty rotten. Although it has been a place I learned to read, a place I came to think, and a place I came to hide.

"My dad died a year and a half ago, and unsurprisingly, things at home have been pretty tricky since then. The nurse's office became like my home. Sarah would feed me. Dash would entertain me. And my teachers would put up with me missing class."

I gulp in air and stare out into the spotlight. I realize the gym has become eerily quiet and that everyone is hanging on my words. I can feel them sticking in my throat and I have to finish quickly, before I can't.

"Hanging out in the nurse's office, I thought I could avoid the world. But, instead, the world came to me. In the shape of a girl named Riley Jackson. Stubborn and funny, Riley has dragged me outside. And made me see what I've been missing. And, in the words of Anne Shirley: 'Kindred spirits are not so scarce as I used to think. It's splendid to find out there are so many of them in the world.'

"I'm not sad to be leaving here. I'll miss Sarah and her morning snacks. I'll miss Ms. Barber and the way she listens. And I'll miss the nurse's office and Dash's jokes and the fridge that hums. But the most important thing I'm taking with me when I leave . . ." I look around to find Riley. I see her standing in front of Ms. Barber, watching me. "My friend . . ."

Riley runs over and hugs me. And I hug her back. Onstage, with all those lights shining bright and all those people staring. In front of us, people are cheering and clapping. Loud, elated clapping, like what I said made sense.

She grins at me. "Do you want to stay and eat burgers?"

I think about it for a second. I'm not scared anymore. And my stomach is churning. And I want to dance with Peggy and laugh with Dash and maybe even introduce Riley to my mum and to Peggy. For once, I'm not ready to go just yet.

"Let's eat. I'm hungry."

"Yeah. Me too," Riley says.

"I'll be back in a second!" I leave Riley on the stage while Mrs. Myer starts thanking various parents for their help with catering and decorating. I hurry down the stairs, skirting along the side of the gym to where I left Mum and Peggy.

"You're still here," I say to Mum.

"Great speech," she says, her eyes shining.

"I love you," I tell her, thinking about how long it's been since I've said it and not been afraid.

"I love you too," she tells me, and reaches out to hug me with force.

Peggy joins in and the three of us rock together in a funny, teary circle in the back corner of the very crowded gym.

Chapter 24

RILEY

IT'S LUNCHTIME AND FOR ONCE I don't have pumpkin soup in a thermos. Mum let me make a sandwich this morning. On whole-grain bread with salad, but still, it's a giant step for her. To be honest, she did go and write down the grams and stick them on a Post-it Note in my lunch bag, but that's okay too.

All around me students rush for the doors, for the sunshine and the games. The mood at school has changed. It's loose and silly, like we're all counting down the final few days and any pretense of working has dropped away. This afternoon we even get to watch a movie with bowls of popcorn Ms. Barber will make in the staff room microwave.

Instead of testing near my locker like I usually do, I grab my lunch and head for the administration building. Sarah looks up and smiles as I sneak down the corridor and through the door.

"You took your time," says Meg, already sitting in her chair.

"Apparently."

She smiles at me and sticks out her feet, flashing her fancy sneakers. "I had PE."

"Did you go?"

She nods. "I beat Nick in a lap of the track. Don't think he could believe it."

I laugh at her, and she brushes her red fringe from her eyes. The color has faded a bit in the past few days but it's still bright. I unzip my lunch bag and then stop. I have to do a test first. Meg watches as I prick the end of my finger.

"Does that hurt?"

"Nah. My fingertips are like sandpaper from all the times I've done this." I hold out my other hand so she can touch the ends of my fingers.

She brushes one of them really lightly.

"Can't even feel that!"

Meg watches as I slide the testing strip into the machine and then smear the drop of blood onto the end. The beep is sharp and I glance down, reading the screen.

"What should the number be?"

"Ideally somewhere between four and eight." I hold it up so she can see the bright blue numbers. "I'm a five today. Mum will be pleased!"

Meg takes out an apple from the brown paper bag she's holding. "Three more days."

"Yeah. It's almost sad."

"Is it?"

"As if. Junior high feels a long way away still," I tell her.

"I'm so ready."

"Helps that you'll be with me!" I say, because we discovered we're going to the same school.

"We can do all our homework together. And have lunch together. And walk to school together," says Meg.

I laugh at that idea. "We might have to convince Mum of the walking part. But one day."

"Hold this," she tells me, handing me her apple.

I watch as she stands up and opens one of the cupboards. She takes something out but I can't see what it is. Then I watch as she rips open a Band-Aid that I assume is for me.

"I don't need one. My finger won't bleed for long," I tell her.

"I know. It's not for you!"

She reaches up and holds down the ripped corner of the Healthy Eating Pyramid poster that looks like it's been on the wall of the nurse's office since the school was built. And then she covers the rip carefully with the Band-Aid.

"I've wanted to do that since the beginning of the year," she says, turning around with a big grin. "I think our time here is done."

"Really? No more nurse's office?"

Meg with a *g* shakes her head. "No. Let's go have lunch outside."

"Yeah."

She packs up her stuff into her paper bag and stands staring at the seat of the chair. She reaches down to touch it. "Goodbye, chair."

"Goodbye, fridge," I say, joining her in touching the furniture.

"Goodbye, Healthy Eating Pyramid poster," she says, waving her hand toward it.

"Goodbye, germy bed," I say.

"Goodbye, nurse's office."

"Yep. Goodbye, nurse's office. And thanks."

Meg lets me go first. I open the door to the corridor without looking back because I know that she's right behind me.

Acknowledgments

It All Begins with Jelly Beans was originally published in Australia as *Sick Bay* in 2018. I first had the idea for this book over five years ago, but the guts of the story kept eluding me. A number of years ago I went to a school camp as the helper for my daughter's friend, Brigid. I learned all about type 1 diabetes in order to be her helper, and we talked a lot about her wish for a book that explained all the complexities of how she felt. Thanks to Brigid and her mum, Siobhan, for their friendship, their honesty, and their insights about type 1 diabetes. Riley and her family are entirely fictional, but without the generous input of Brigid and Siobhan, they would never have come to life.

It's been a dream of mine to have one of my books published in the US, and I feel very lucky to have found a home at Simon & Schuster for *It All Begins with Jelly Beans*. A huge thanks to my amazing agent, Allison Hellegers, and to everyone at Stimola Literary Agency for making this happen. Given how awful last year was, this feels like an absolute gift.

Thanks to editor Kate Prosswimmer for being so enthusiastic and supportive of this book. And thanks to illustrator Federica Frenna for the gorgeous cover illustration, associate editor Nicole Fiorica, designer Rebecca Syracuse, managing editor Bridget Madsen, proofreader Mandy Veloso, and all at Simon & Schuster for bringing this book to life.

A huge thanks to Christina Collins for her lovely words on the cover.

Writing about friendship is my happy place, and I have to thank some pretty extraordinary friends who pulled me through this tricky year: Saurenne Deleuil, for always being at the end of a phone when I need her; Emily Gale, for being the best early reader and coconspirator a girl could have; Tina Valentine, Jo Kasch, and Emma Eastman, for just being there; and my weekly coffee posse of Kathryn, Bridget, Lisa, Meredith, Gabi, Amanda, Kathy, Jodie, Lynda, and Sophie, for making Wednesdays so joyful. As I get older it's pretty clear that everything is made infinitely better by the wonderful women I know, and I feel very lucky to have you all in my life.

And finally, thanks to my partner, Aidan, and our kids, Evie and Arlo, for all the love, the mess, and the joy.